D0812324

HEART FAILURES

By Ursula Perrin

GHOSTS

HEART FAILURES

URSULA PERRIN

Heart Failures

1978
Doubleday & Company, Inc.
Garden City, New York

ASBURY PARK PUBLIC LIBRARY
ASBURY PARK, NEW JERSEY

Library of Congress Cataloging in Publication Data
Perrin, Ursula, 1935–
Heart failures.
I. Title.
PZ4.P4585He [PS3566.E6944] 813'.5'4
ISBN: 0-385-14170-X
Library of Congress Catalog Card Number 78–52111

COPYRIGHT © 1978 BY URSULA PERRIN
ALL RIGHTS RESERVED
PRINTED IN THE UNITED STATES OF AMERICA
FIRST EDITION

For Mark

"Heart failure represents an inability of the heart to maintain an adequate output . . . When the heart fails, a variety of compensations are evoked which tend to restore this vital function."

Diseases of the Heart
Charles K. Friedberg

ONE

1.

An Eden? Well, not exactly, I think, and sleepily reach for a cigarette. Coming back from the hospital, I drove, she talked, and now she is still talking. Not about her husband. About our upstate childhood.

"But, Nell," she says again, "it was, you know, a sort of, oh, Eden."

Coming back from the hospital everything was black, a sodden night with mist rolling before the headlights. Even here in my living room, the atmosphere is ambiguous. The smoke from our cigarettes gently rises and just one lamp is on. Carrie sits in its half-light. Shoes off, she is curled up into a sofa corner, a large woman with gestures a little too girlish. Is she acting? I am. After all these years, I am not very glad to see her.

"Now of course," Carrie says, "by the time a girl's twenty-one or -two, she's done it all. *Every*thing. The TV, the movies, those awful magazines they sell everywhere. When I was that age I was, well, unsophisticated."

Were you? I think. Not me. That summer we were fourteen, I *knew*. Oh no, not Eden. Not a paradise. Good and bad, like any place. What time is it? Past two? How long will she stay? A week? And now tomorrow's shot, dammit. I hate Sundays when Jack's not here. Damned moody Irishman, taking off like that. "Shaughnessy means wanderer," he said once, "in Gaelic." Eternally wandering we were, too. Half my childhood Sundays spent driving. After church, a roast chicken and the New York *Times*, we'd "go for a nice Sunday drive," over the dun-colored back roads of desolate upstate New York. And only at the top of Hill Street, a glance at the house behind two tall shaggy hemlocks, my favorite house, a solid gray fieldstone house with two chimneys, a "Dutch" roof, white window trim, black shutters . . .

"Because, Nell," says Carrie, "I wanted to keep my kids from all that. I think that today more than ever kids need that sort of foundation. A place where they can feel safe. I wanted to give them an old-fashioned sort of family life, a strong sense of home . . ."

. . . a handsome house that would have seemed remote except for diverse traces of human occupancy—beneath the hemlocks a bicycle left on its side like a wounded deer, one delicate pedal still spinning in the air, or in winter the sudden insulting plop of a snowball landing just on the other side of the glass from your face and the figure that rose to heave it now (as the snow slowly insultingly slid off the window) plainly rising, hooting with laughter, running away, and in summer as you passed, leaning out of the open car window with your chin in the warm crease of your folded arm, the muted growl of a lawn mower and sudden icy shrieks as two kids about your age, girls, barefoot and in shorts, come running between the hemlocks: one stops, goes rigid with delight and ecstatically screams as the other turns the garden sprinkler on. Loudonville, Minnaville, Altaville, Plainville . . .

. . . "security," Carrie says. "That starts at home. With the parents, of course. Their—all right, I'll use that old-fashioned word—morality. Their . . ."

. . . St. Jamesville, Westville, Northville, Mayville. Up and down steep, steeper hills, staunch little white clapboard houses clamped to the stony hillsides, fields, stubbled in fall, dotted white with buckwheat in the spring, barns, mostly broken-down, sheds, lean-tos, cows, boredom. Taffy, the cocker spaniel, sidling closer and closer to you on the back seat and finally, raising dark-centered chocolate eyes with an expression that says, "Forgive me, Nell," vomiting. Time to stop, clean car, run dog. The afternoon is swiftly going.

Right about here, your father gets lost. Dr. Dreher's mouth is shut in a hard line and he ignores Mrs. Dreher, who is never lost, who has every rock and spruce and clump of birches memorized. She says to him crossly, in English, "You should have gone left at that last little side road." He says nothing, continues on; now they are really lost, the day wanes. Mrs. Dreher says, in a German as stiff with thorns as the print in your old Grimm's fairy tale book, "Johann, can't you see this is not the right way? Do you live only behind the walls of your mind?"

"Ah yes," he says in German, cheerfully sarcastic, "but the walls of my mind are hung with interesting pictures."

Pink twilight falls on upstate New York. For some time now, Nell has had to go to the bathroom. She sits with her thighs pinched together. The car stinks of Taffy's vomit. At last they are back on Hill Street, the quivering nose of the car pointed down toward the town, the valley, the river. In summer the air has a thick, rose-gold bloom of dust; in winter, the cold car's air tastes thinly metallic, pink and silver. Lamps are going on. They pass the house. Behind its hemlocks every window is lit.

Her mother says, "Look at those lights! Just think of their electric bill."

Her father says, sarcastically, "Our town's leading surgeon! Perhaps he's not home. They say he's stingy, Van Duyne."

But Nell, thinking of the house behind them, imagines the life going on inside its walls—a house full of children, where interesting things are always happening. The house is very old, so much a part of the hill, the town, the town's past, it's as if the house were a natural thing—rooted, just as she thinks of the Van Duynes as rooted, here in Veddersburg, New York (pop. 28,000) forever, yesterday, today, tomorrow—while they, the Drehers, are somehow itinerants, wandering, just the three of them (and Taffy), through the world.

"Nonsense," her mother says. "In Germany, you have hundreds of relatives. It was just because of the war." In her broad white forehead, her swift black brows droop into a V, like gull's wings quickly sketched. Then these brows soar up and she says, looking at Nell with her gray intelligent eyes, "Besides, we are all wanderers."

We are?

Yes.

How come?

Because. When Adam and Eve sinned, they were expelled from the Garden of Eden, from Paradise. Ever since, mankind has wandered, looking for home.

But nobody wanders, that I know. Except us. We're always moving. We're the only ones who ever move.

Wandering in a different sense. A spiritual sense. You see, we are looking . . .

Margarete Dreher stops, frowns. She is conventionally religious, her grandfather was a minister, she believes in religion as a restraint on the evils of the human spirit (but in fact, she doubts, and later in her life, she says one day, quite simply, "I can no longer believe in God."). We are looking, she says firmly, for a spiritual home.

Home to Nell meant not so much one of the Drehers' various houses as the gray fieldstone house at the top of Hill Street. Even before she knew them, she wanted to love the Van Duynes, and sometimes at night as she lay in bed and listened to her parents' voices on the other side of the door she imagined herself a part of that other family.

. . . "so that," says Carrie, "when I think of old-fashioned family life and old-fashioned character, I think of the Van Duynes. Don't you?"

2.

I had gotten up Saturday morning feeling low, with all sorts of evil presentiments. Saturdays when I'm on call I wish to God I'd chosen a different sort of life. It's a pain to go to the office and know that Jack's in New York, restlessly glooming around and that when I finish the day at midnight or so he'll call me in a surly mood, feeling cheated out of half his weekend. I keep feeling guilty about my life, keep trying to make it up to him. Do men physicians feel this way? Nonsense. Take my colleague down the hall, Dr. Bodine (who, when I first started in practice, would patronizingly call me Nelly in front of my patients). Vic Bodine doesn't feel guilty: he leaves both his wife and mistress alone most of the time. Were all the women of my generation brought up to believe so resolutely that they must fill in the margins of a man's life? Those awful movies of the forties and fifties wherein the career "gal" takes off her glasses, lets down her hair, gives up her job and lo! becomes a real woman. Out that gal went to the suburbs, with kids, mugs of coffee, picture windows, and generally lobotomized living, which brings me to Mrs. Callister, my first patient of the day, Room 401, eighty-three and senile, who fell out of her hospital bed last night. It's a mystery to me how she got out of her restraints. I suspect an overeager son or daughter-in-law untied them, hoping the old lady would land on her skull, which is ninety percent full of hardened arteries. Unfortunately, it was her hip she broke, which will mean a long, long hospital stay, more money, a nursing home—God grant me a swift end and no lengthy babbling decline. On I went to Room 404, Mrs. McMillen, who ever since the first day she saw me has been threatening to sue me for "malfeasance." She had been caught at 3 A.M. in the ward supply room, stuffing her Bloomingdale's shopping bag full of hospital sheets and towels. It's hard for me to deal kindly with her, plainly a nut and a larcenous one, but with the kind of virtuous blue eyes that juries always go for. By the time I got to the office there were eight people waiting, six of whom had just read the latest New York *Times* series on the conspiracy of American physicians to kill off most of the American population while simultaneously picking their pockets. Aside from the New Jersey State Lottery, "sue" is the last frontier, the last chance to make it big. No wonder "sue" stands out in everybody's eyes these days the way it was once oil in Texas or gold in Alaska. Patients that hadn't read the New York *Times* had read the *Reader's Digest* and were all upset about pollution and cancer. As well they should be, only fifty years too late. God knows why I live in New Jersey, the most crowded, neurotic, polluted, corrupt, carcinogenic state in the Union, with no traditions or character, only lots of six-lane highways and fast food places. The state is a mess. I'm here I guess because it's close to New York and when I divorced James Calverson, I thought I wanted to be near his kids—of whom I had grown very fond. Their mother, Jim's first wife, then promptly remarried and took the kids to San Francisco, so there I was, family-less again.

Saturday went on, full of more bad than good. The report on Kathy Harrington came in, little Kathy whom I helped get into nursing school. She's twenty-two and pregnant, but not a word about marriage, of course. I know what this means. Her mother will raise the kid—if she lives that long, since Stella Harrington has a bad heart. These kids astound me. They won't use contraceptives, they are anti-abortion, they treat babies as if they were delightful toys and, like the children they themselves are, drop these toys when they are tired of playing.

Years ago, during my second awful marriage, when I was trying so hard to get pregnant, I used to take the bus up First Avenue in New York. At Bellevue Hospital hoards of mothers would get on, in all shapes, sizes, colors, trailing children like streamers, and I would wonder why I couldn't have a baby when all the rest of the world was so casually fecund. Thank God that Jack has Tim and Laura by his first marriage, nice kids they are, too, though this time I am more cautious, armoring myself against making those attachments, which may eventually hurt, when broken. Jack and I are like a fond elderly couple, with his apartment in New York, my house out here, the brick terrace he's been slowly putting in, the pool, the garden, Hetty, the cleaning lady, little trips to interesting places, the theater. With two incomes there's enough money, although of course Jack pays Nancy alimony and child support. That in itself no small reason why I didn't instantly accept his first "proposition."

At nine o'clock I was still in the hospital and they were—relentlessly—paging me. I picked up the phone on the fourth floor:

"Dr. Calverson."

"Dr. Calverson, I'm here at your house cooking dinner. Where the hell are you?"

"Mr. Shaughnessy," I said, "how nice of you to call, but I'm on my way out with a stud. We're going to a motel on Route 22 for an orgy." Sarah Ennis, a steely-eyed head nurse raised her white-capped head and stared through her glittering glasses. How unprofessional of me.

"No kidding," Jack said. "I thought you might be home for dinner, love."

I hate it when Jack does this to me. He knew I'd be working today and now he's letting me know I've gypped him.

"Sorry," I said briskly, "but I've got to wait here for a patient."

He began to wheedle. "And I cooked you a lovely little dinner, love, rice with veal piccata and a salad." I do so love to watch Jack cook. He lines up every herb in the kitchen and, whistling all the while, throws in a bit of this and a bit of that.

"I'll try to get home by ten. Have a bottle of beer and relax."

"I've already had three bottles of beer, Doctor. I'll tell you what I'm going to do, Doctor. If you're not home in half an hour I'm going to masturbate over the veal."

I slid my hand over the mouthpiece for the sake of old Ennis, whose bent lined neck was turning a mottled red. "Oh?" I said. "Well, save some for me."

I think the reason I like Jack Shaughnessy so much is that he can always make me smile.

When I finally did get home—it was 11:05—Jack's car wasn't in the drive. Gone for more beer, I thought, but stuck under the front-door knocker was a folded note, and standing in my dimlit living room, I read, "See you soon." I could see that the kitchen was ominously neat. The telephone rang. It was Mrs. Moscowitz reporting in garbled fashion that her husband was unconscious on the bathroom floor. I told her I would get an ambulance, put Jack's note down on the table and left for the hospital, glad to be out of my pretty little house, which seemed now filled with Jack's absence and loneliness.

When I got back to the hospital, an ambulance—not mine —was already there, accompanied by two policemen. Police sergeant Matt Gambino was standing at the information desk filling out a report, his holster slung under that belly I kid him about. My patient hadn't yet come in. The other, younger, policeman was going through a wallet, looking for identification. "Dr. Richard A. Kurtz," he announced to Gambino. "Forty-one Eastwood Drive, Ellerton, New Jersey."

Gambino grunted. I glanced toward the stretcher at the other end of the room and glanced away. One of the interns started an IV and Sally Eustace, the emergency room nurse, came to the desk and put in a page for Claude Pappas, the neurosurgeon.

I glanced at the stretcher again. It couldn't be. Could it?

"Where did it happen?" I asked Matt. "Route 22?"

"Two eighty-seven," he said. "We haven't exactly gotten the picture yet. The girl with him died."

Behind a hastily put-up screen there was another stretcher in the room, which everyone kept avoiding.

"Jesus," Matt said, "I wish to God I didn't know her mother."

I had a terrible foreboding and I went over to the stretcher that already seemed so abandoned, like a thing you just throw away, and I flipped down enough of the blanket to see what was left of Kathy Harrington's face. There was a huge darkening bloody hole from her left temple to her jaw so that nothing on that side of her face was recognizable. Black blood matted her fine blond hair. Her right blue eye stared up at me, the fluorescent lights, nothing. I covered her face and looked at the other stretcher. In the space between Sally Eustace and little Dr. Puchero, the surgical resident, I saw—this time for sure—the noble profile of Richard A. Kurtz, MD, my first husband. Long ago I had loved him and slept in his bed.

"Hi, Matt," the young policeman said. "You want to call this guy's wife?"

"Are you kidding?" Matt said. "Why would I want to call her?"

Through the windows of the emergency room doors I could see the flashing red beam of another ambulance arriving. A nurse pulled back the doors. Four Summerville residents, volunteers in white jump suits, came in carrying my patient on a stretcher. Old Mrs. Moscowitz followed them in, looking around with dazed light-struck eyes. "He had a terrible headache, Doctor," she said, "and I said to him, 'Ben, why doncha take two aspirin?' And he took 'em and just fell over. Was it the aspirin, Doctor? Did I tell him the wrong thing? Why did this have to happen to me now? We were goin' on a cruise, we were goin' to Bermuda. I never in my whole life been to Bermuda."

The girl at the desk continued to type out forms and the switchboard operator paged Claude Pappas and Matt Gambino put in a call to Carrie Pettigrew Kurtz in Ellerton, New Jersey.

"But we were lucky, Nell, don't you think so?" Carrie is saying. "To have had them, the Van Duynes, especially Mrs. Van
Duyne—Rhee. I was crazy about her when I was a kid, adored
her. I wanted to be just like her. I suppose being only children,
you and I needed that—another house to go to, full of—oh—
life, fun, activity. Some mornings now I wake up at home and
it sounds like the Van Duyne house to me and I think, I've accomplished that, anyway. Do you remember the noises? Julia
was always upstairs playing the flute and Buzz and Clay out in
the yard fighting about the barn doors—Buzz wanted them
down so that he could hit tennis balls and Clay wanted them
up so that he could see to work on one of his motors. And
Peter. Do you remember the noises from Peter's room? That
bubbling sound from the fish tanks and the animals all squeak-
ing and scrabbling their claws against the wire cages. I wonder
what Peter's doing now. Do you think he's a biologist? Do you
remember the time Mina let all of his animals out?"

"God, yes," I say. "We were in the eighth grade. She went
to the movies with someone—who was it?"

"Billy Morrison," Carrie says. "I remember because I had
such a crush on him."

"That's right, it was Billy. They were up in the second row
of the balcony necking and Peter spied on them and told Dr.
Van Duyne. Mina was furious."

"So she went up to his room and let out all the animals.

The cat got two of the white mice, and Peter cried and cried."

"She could be cruel," I say.

"Yes," Carrie says, "there was a sort of watchfulness about her. She wanted to see what would happen next, how you'd react. I thought she was often cold."

"I don't know," I say. "I don't think cold, really. Cool. That was her defense, don't you think so?"

"Defense? Against what? With Rhee Van Duyne for a mother?"

"But we all have defenses," I say gently.

"The fact is," Carrie goes on, hardly listening (I have seen this before, this outpouring of talk in the midst of a crisis), "we had a lovely time, didn't we? I do think of that time as a sort of Eden, a paradise. Maybe that's why I haven't been back. Not for fifteen years anyhow, not since Dad moved down to Florida. All my roots are in Ellerton now. Oh. The tree house. Remember our tree house? I never did understand why you two burned it down. Remember when Peter climbed up to the tree house and fell? I thought he was dead, he lay on the ground so quietly." She stops, the word "dead" has amazed her. She lifts her face, sighs, goes on. "I've tried to give my children something of what they had, that sort of family life. I hope I've accomplished that. I think I have. We've been lucky, of course. Until tonight." Her head drops on her folded fist, and the lamplight picks up silver glints in her pile of brown and gray-streaked hair. She is sitting in a corner of my sofa with her shoes off and her feet curled up under her. It is 3 A.M. this rainy September Sunday. Phil, her sixteen-year-old son, is asleep in my guest room.

"Carrie," I say, "let's talk about Dick, all right? I think if we talked about it, it would be better."

"All right," she says practically, lifting her head.

"I have to say this, Carrie—he might not make it. Right now the object is to keep him breathing. He's on that cooling mattress you saw, to help keep the swelling down so that pressure doesn't increase on the breathing center. If it looks like his neurological signs are deteriorating, they'll operate. I want you to know that Claude Pappas, the neurosurgeon, is absolutely first-rate. There just isn't anybody better. Still, if they operate and he survives, it'll be a long hard haul. He may wake up fairly soon, he may be in a coma for quite a while. Neurologically, we won't really know what the score is till much later. You see, with a child the recuperative process in brain swelling is faster. With an adult . . ."

"He's strong," Carrie says. "Physically, he's a marvelous specimen." Is there a trace of irony in her voice?

"He's forty-six," I say. "What I'm trying to tell you is that if he lives he may not be himself again."

"I see."

"Everything—breathing, eyesight, speech, movement—depends upon the good health of the brain. Right now, we're only at step number one: survival."

She says nothing.

I say, "You must be exhausted. I really think you should get some rest."

She gets up slowly. "You're so kind to do this, Nell. After all these years—seventeen years. Funny the way things turn out, isn't it?"

At the door to the den—I have made up the sofa bed for her—she stops and looks over her shoulder at me, a large woman with tired blue eyes. "Is it hard for you, Nell, living alone?"

I am caught off guard—Carrie, who never said anything tactless, who never asked personal questions—and I answer rather dryly, "Only sometimes," and she nods and says good night and closes the door.

4.

I hadn't liked Jack Shaughnessy the first time I met him. I'm a sucker for the long, lean Anglo-Saxon type and he just wasn't it at all: only a couple of inches taller than I, squarely built with a budding paunch, a square-jawed passive face, dark, dark red hair, and God, freckles even. He didn't have a brogue or Irish wit but sat watching me across the restaurant table in a sort of glum reverie. His eyes were brown with gold lights in them. I talked to the others for a while, and after two margaritas and two glasses of red wine, leaned toward him and said in a whisper, "Are you shy?"

"No," he said in an ordinary voice, "I'm tired."

All evening, this was all he said. He called me the next night and asked if I'd like to go to dinner.

"No," I said, "I think not."

"Why not?" he asked. Obviously not shy.

"Because," I said, "I'll be too tired to do all the talking."

"Maybe we can be tired together."

I ignored the innuendo, if there was one, and said, "Mr. Shaughnessy, you strike me as one of those gentlemen who thinks a female should be decorative and entertaining. Have you ever considered a geisha? Frankly, Mr. Shaughnessy, I work terribly hard and I sometimes like my males to entertain me." There was a pause and a click. He had hung up. A half hour later the phone rang again.

"How about this?" he said. "I'll get two tickets for *Grease*."

"I've seen it," I said, only by now beginning to be a little intrigued, he was so persistent.

"So have I," he said. "We could nap through it and then maybe later entertain each other. If we felt strong enough."

"I don't think so," I said. "I hate nostalgia, I hated the fifties, and this sounds like a proposition. I never accept propositions on first dates."

"Oh, dammit!" he suddenly bellowed, and hung up.

When the telephone rang again I thought it was Shaughnessy, and I answered it by saying, "Look, I've got an idea," but instead of Jack there was a puzzled pause at the other end of the line and an ancient reedy voice croaked, "Is this Dr. Calverson?" After that, two more phone calls—one from the hospital, one from Mrs. Battaglia, who had shingles. At 10 P.M. I called New York City information. No, I told the operator, I had no address for him. In a trochee-accented singsong voice she said, "There are twenty-one John Shaughnessys in Manhattan." I hung up, poured myself a very small glass of Grand Marnier and watched part of the Carol Burnett show. When the telephone rang I jumped to get it but it was the hospital wanting a clarification of some orders. At eleven I took a bath and at midnight went to bed. What a stable, orderly life I lead. At twelve-thirty my doorbell rang. I went out to the living room, snapping on lights all the way, and opened the door a crack, leaving the chain secured. I wasn't expecting burglars but New Jersey is full of lunatics. In my haste, I dropped my bathrobe tie and I stood at the door, one hand on the knob, the other clutching my bunched robe together.

"How about this?" Jack Shaughnessy said. "Two tickets for a production of Uncle Vanya right out here in New Jersey."

I said wildly, "I'm not dressed."

"So I see," he said. "But the tickets aren't for tonight. Do you think you could let me in? It's raining."

I stared at him.

"For Christ's sake, will you open the goddam door?" he shouted. "I'm wet as a snake and catching pneumonia."

Among other things, he was a hypochondriac. He came right in, grumbling and complaining, hung his sodden London Fog in my closet and went out to the kitchen, where, suddenly whistling, he filled up the teakettle and put it on. "Pretty cold for June," he said, rubbing his blunt red hands. "Would you have any bread? I somehow neglected to eat dinner. What's that stuff on your face? It won't help, you know. I once wrote an article on cold creams. Sheer waste of money."

I said dryly that I used Ponds, which wouldn't exactly break my piggy bank.

He said—pouring out two cups of tea—that he could tell right away I was what men ("forgive me") called a cockteaser—a very attractive woman who (he went on) turned into a practical no-nonsense asexual female robot the minute anyone got interested.

Nothing flatters a woman more than an analysis—however inaccurate—of her personality. Tell her she is lovely-looking and she will feel a hot threatening hand upon her thigh, but convey to her that she is interesting and you've got one hand in her pants. We had tea and toast together at 1 A.M. (suddenly I was ravenously hungry), by 2 he had told me one version, condensed, of his life's story, by 3 we were drinking our tea with rum and holding hands across the kitchen table. I told him in three sentences about my first two disastrous marriages and at 4 A.M., when the black weight of night had ever so gently lifted at the edges, and eastward, toward the city, a ragged margin of pink appeared, we went to the bedroom. He was more nervous than I and kept bumping into things—"Ow, dammit,"—and modestly turned his back as he dropped his pants. How can you feel threatened by a man that makes you smile? His upper back, chest and arms were covered by light, reddish, curling hair which turned darker on his buttocks. I lay under the sheet, naked and smiling. He edged into bed sideways, trying to keep his hand cupped over an enormous blushing erection. His pubic hair resembled live copper wires.

"You know," I said as he slid under the sheet, "you shouldn't be so modest. Lots of men have trouble getting that vertical."

"Do you think," he complained, "that for just a few minutes you could forget your MD degree and remember what sex you are?" He turned on his side toward me, looking pale and serious. We lay somewhat apart, not touching, then his foot found mine.

"Oh Christ, I knew it," he said, closing his eyes. "Ice-cold and here it is summer."

"I have a very warm heart," I said, and took his hand and put it on my breast, and silvery gray light filled my long glass windows and outside and inside everything began to come alive, alive.

Sunday, 9 A.M. I wake up all at once knowing that Kurtz is in the hospital, Carrie is in my house, Jack isn't beside me and the telephone, the telephone is ringing.

"Nell?" It's Claude Pappas, the neurosurgeon. "Listen, we're going to operate on your friend Kurtz." I talk to Pappas briefly and have just put down the phone when it rings again. This time it's a person named George Smythe, calling from Ellerton, New Jersey. He is the Kurtzs' insurance agent. I say, "My, you guys are speedy." He says, taking offense, "I'd like to speak to Mrs. Kurtz." I try being nicer, more soothing and professional, and explain that we are just leaving, Mrs. Kurtz and I, for the hospital, that Dr. Kurtz is about to go into surgery, that I am an old family friend.

"I see," he says, replying to my courteous professional tone with his own variation. "I—uh—understand there was another person involved in the accident?" Yes, I say, that's correct. "She's—uh—deceased?" Yes, I say, and then a funny thing happens. A human quality, a softening of timbre, comes into Mr. George Smythe's voice and he says, "Dr. Calverson, I've known Mrs. Kurtz for a long time. We're neighbors. Our kids have grown up together. Would you do me a favor? Tell her about the girl as kindly as you can. She's . . . a lovely woman. She doesn't deserve this. And tell her soon, before someone else does."

I hang up and lie back in bed, looking out the glass windows. My little house is built in the shape of an "L" and every room has long sliding glass doors that open out to the pool. Outside, the sky has a pale opal luster with bits of real blue in it and every once in a while the sun comes out and the drenched shrubbery, green and glossy rhododendrons, andromedas, mountain laurels, glistens briefly. I suddenly resent Kurtz coming back into my life this way. I don't want to think about him, I want Jack and I want to be in my garden. I hear water running in the guest bath, and when I step into the hall I almost fall over Phil, who is coming out of the bathroom, and the unexpectedness of it and the fact that he looks very much like his father startles me: same prominent nose, same slanting fall of hair, same hooded deep-set eyes, but with Carrie's long mouth and shy smile.

"Gee, I didn't mean to scare you," he says, looking down at me from his sixteen-year-old height. "I hope you don't mind, but I used the razor in there."

"Sure, that's fine. Do I smell coffee?"

He nods and smiles his old man's crooked, charming smile. "Hope I did the coffee okay. I just started drinking coffee a couple of weeks ago. I never liked the flavor before."

"Life is full of things you grow up to," I say. Sententious old Dr. Calverson. Jesus, lady, they ought to give you your own TV show. He kindly ignores my TV psychologist personality and asks about his father. When I tell him he frowns and turns away.

I knock on the door to the den and then go in when Carrie doesn't respond. She is sleeping soundly, her left arm straight up under the pillow and her hand dangling uncomfortably. She has long hands, not graceful, with the nails chipped in many places. I gently press her shoulder. In sleep she least of all resembles her childhood self, that pale, square-faced, serious little girl.

"Oh!" she says, her eyes opening suddenly. "What is it?"

"Good morning," I say, and sit down on the edge of the bed. She stares at me and struggles out of sleep, then sits up, pulling the pillow up behind her. She had gone to sleep in her slip but had removed the bra, and the sight of her large freckled shoulders and large loose braless bosom, the nipples dark against the inset lace, is somehow touching. Her slip is carefully made, one of those expensive French numbers that I thought women last wore in the 1930's. Did Dick buy it for her?

"What time is it?"

"A little after nine."

"I ought to call home."

"Carrie, Dr. Pappas called. He's going to operate on Dick."

Her eyes look suddenly shocked and then she frowns. "I see. Well, in that case, I'd better get dressed. Is Phil up?"

"Your dear son made some coffee. What a nice boy he is."

She sighs, looks out of the window, then reaches for the chair where she had dropped her bra and I see with surprise that it too is carefully made and lacy—a little 40E something I am sure no man would ever buy his wife. It strikes me as sad and amusing that she has this thing for underwear but maybe that's just me, my own preference being the cheapest and most utilitarian kind. She says so softly I almost don't hear, "I love him so much," and I smile, thinking she means her son Phil, but closing the door, think that perhaps she means Kurtz, and then it occurs to me that sometime soon I am going to have to tell her about Kathy Harrington.

At one o'clock I go back up to the fourth floor and the OR. The light above Pappas' room is off, and just then Claude comes out into the hall in his street clothes, a handsome gray pin-striped suit.

"Kurtz made it," he says, looking cheerful. "And it looks as if I'm going to make Sunday dinner for the first time in two months. Elsie will be pleased."

Claude is a small, wiry, balding man with dark Byzantine eyes straight out of an icon. He reminds me of the Pantokrator you see in Greek churches but the OR nurses complain that in the operating room he acts like the God of the Old

Testament—all thunder and lightning. Socially, he's mild-mannered, but he can unleash curses you've never heard while operating and has been known to throw out assistants, students, nurses, anyone who didn't shape up. He's a perfectionist—a good thing to be in his line of work, or maybe in any line of demanding work. There's another thing about Claude—he has a conscience. He doesn't operate so much for the fee as for the benefit of the patient and the exercise of his own skill, which is considerable.

"So," he says, walking down the hall next to me with his springy step, "your friend Kurtz is holding his own."

I say, "He's not my friend, Claude. He's an ex-husband."

"No kidding," Claude says, "that's interesting. I've met him, you know. He gave a paper on hepatic coma at an American Surgical Society meeting a year or so ago. It was a darn good paper. He's a good man."

"He's a smart man," I say, correcting Claude.

"Hmm," Claude says, "do I detect a little—er—rancor in your voice?"

"Not at all," I say. "It's been a long time since I was married to that bastard. I was thinking just now, though, that maybe instead of getting you on the case I should have gotten Donaldson." Claude laughs, showing small white teeth.

"Remind me sometime," he says, "to tell you the latest Donaldson story."

"You know, Claude," I say, "I don't think I want to hear it. I haven't gotten over last summer yet. Remember? When you went to Europe and Donaldson covered for you? How did we avoid a suit on that case?"

"Don't make me feel guilty, Nell," he says, taking my elbow. "I've got to get out of here once in a while. Besides, if I brought him up to the committee, wouldn't they think I was trying to get a competitor? Tell me about Kurtz. If he's your ex, what's your current connection to him?"

"There isn't any. I was in the emergency room when they

brought him in. We split a long, long time ago. After we divorced he married a childhood friend of mine."

"Mrs. Kurtz is a friend of yours?" he says, getting it all straight. "I guess I'd better go see her. Does she know about the—uh—other victim?"

"No."

"Kurtz is a bit of a philanderer?"

"I haven't seen him for seventeen years, Claude. I really don't know what he's like now. When I was married to him he wasn't so nice. It wasn't . . . philandering, it was . . . Oh hell. I find even now I don't want to talk about it."

Claude shakes his head, smiling. I can see he doesn't believe me. "You know, Nell, I can't help but admire these guys. Where do they get the time? And the energy! The act, itself, is nothing, it's the peripheral circumstance—the planning, the slyness, the deception." He sighs. "The point is, if I went out of my way for a little *amour*, Elsie would know instantly and she'd be sore as hell. Now I hate to make Elsie mad. It throws off the meals, for one thing. You know? Instead of getting a nice home-cooked dinner you're suddenly dispatched to a diner on Route 22. And I really don't function well on diner food. So what it comes down to is this, in order to practice my profession I have to stay on the straight and narrow."

"Claude, you're lucky, you know that? What you're not saying is that you and Elsie get along just fine."

"Lots of people get along fine, Nell. Sometimes that's not the point. Look at your friend Mrs. Kurtz. I can take one look at her and tell you that she's a lovely woman. Am I right?"

"Probably. She used to be a lovely girl."

I go down the hall to the Ladies' Room to give Claude time to speak to Carrie. Passing the mirror over the sink, I see a face that shocks me. Overnight the lines in my face have deepened. Dummy, I think, Jack may be last-chanceville and here you are passing him up. Where is he today? Probably gone up to Larchmont to spend the day with his kids. Nancy

would be there, of course. I'd never met his ex-wife but knew
I had feelings about her. *She* had left *him*. I wish it had been
the other way around, but wait a minute; no, I don't. Jack
wouldn't have left his kids, and underneath his gloom and ir-
reverence and eccentricities and hypochondria it seems to me
there is something steady and strong there, something that I
admire and need, and yet—what is it I'm afraid of? I've been
married to two other men—Kurtz, a charming bastard, and
Calverson, a prig, but they had been alike in one way. Both
times, the marriage, our marriage, had really been their marriage. They hadn't cared if I did my little thing—medicine—as
long as they weren't inconvenienced. When I married Kurtz,
I was a third-year medical student and he was a resident in
gastroenterology, already doing extensive research on liver disease. I thought this marriage was going to work out real fine,
we had so much to talk about. But whenever we got into a
professional discussion, he had a certain way he used to fix his
face—oh, nothing really condescending, just the merest sug-
gestion of a smile, and then, by and by, he began to say, only
half kidding, "Are you sure you want to stay in medicine?"

So, in my second marriage, I was careful to select a mate
with a completely different career. James Calverson, of the
Maryland Calversons, was in the bond market. He played
both sides of the game, showing me off to his friends as if I
were a curiosity and at the same time taking credit for having
married this bright woman, with the implication, of course,
that he was at least as smart (he wasn't). But when we went
out, I quickly got the clue that my place as ever was with the
ladies, who were all at that point decorating apartments and
having babies. I was not to embarrass him by being too intelligent. So I'd sit with the ladies, discussing Junior's formula
and giving vague advice on diet and vitamins, and I even let
them know, batting my eyelashes, that Jim and I were, you
know, trying, and so got their sympathy; it made me one of
the girls that we, too, were "trying." So much for the weekend. Weeknights I only had to have dinner ready at the usual

time (he got home two hours before I did), and pick up on
the six days Lulu didn't clean, and Saturday mornings while
he slept shop for food, and Saturday afternoons while he
played squash visit the laundromat, and he liked fresh flowers
nicely arranged on the table, and we had to do some entertaining, and also, I was to keep myself looking acceptable,
which meant the hairdresser, and now we come back to the
guilt question, feel sorry for *him* when I was on duty at night.
Because, after all, I was leaving him all alone. He never complained, oh no, nothing so gross, there was only the very
slightest resigned set to his jaw when I showed up the next
day to cook his dinner, and only the very tiniest flicker of im-
patience in the small muscles around his eyes when I got too
interested in one of my cases. Why did I marry him? I was
lonely. Why did he marry me? I never did figure that one
out. I think he married me to spite his mother.

My time with Shaughnessy has never been like that, but for
one thing, we're not married. Besides, it's a positive benefit to
him that I'm a doctor. First of all, because he's such a
hypochondriac—I'm a walking set of medical references—and
secondly, he's a writer and I function for him the way a peri-
scope does for a submarine—I let him know what's going on
out there, and Christ, it's been a good combination. I must be
crazy not to marry him. Do I really want to spend the rest of
my life alone?

"You know something?" Carrie says, "I'm really crazy about
this house. I never thought I'd like a modern house."

"Thanks," I say. "You want the magazine section?"

"No, thanks," she says, "I've seen it. My house is ninety
years old, a rambling broken-down Victorian."

"I can just see it," I say. "Eight bedrooms and a conserva-
tory."

"Eight bedrooms and a sun porch," she says, "and stop
sounding so snide. The upkeep is exhausting, but despite the

cranky plumbing and wiring, Victorian houses are great. They have lots of character."

"So do the people who run them," I say, "or they soon acquire it. Lord, I'll bet you have dogs, too. Let me guess: a lab and a golden retriever."

"You are being snide. Just remember that we can't all be glamorous lady physicians."

I laugh. Is she teasing or flattering me? A little of both, maybe. She recognizes that I'm not in the best of moods. Her presence here (Phil has gone home) disrupts my Sunday schedule, which is to sit silently out here and read. I crave this weekly peace, a deep golden pool of quiet time. When Jack is here he sits just a few feet off, reading, his horn-rims comically crooked, occasionally clearing his throat and turning a page.

Carrie gets up from the chaise. Her blue denim wrap skirt divides, showing a pie-shaped slice of white thigh. "I know I shouldn't, but I think I'll have another piece of cake. Can I get some for you?" I shake my head, no. One thing I've already learned about Carrie is that she eats too much.

It interests me that often, in someone you knew years ago, a little theme emerges to dominate what was at twenty a fluid movement of personality: irony, bitterness, aggression, greed —these themes work themselves out in a person's face and body. Irony shows itself in that crooked hardness around the mouth, resignation in the down-droop of the facial muscles, greed in that tightness around the eyes that comes from continually squinting to assess the worth of other people's possessions. Carrie puzzles me. She's a large woman with an ample bosom, no waist and long thin legs. Her lashes and eyebrows, always pale, look lightly flecked with dust and her eyes, once a bright blue, are lighter. She has a comfortable, ready laugh and a kind, patient look, but every so often there is a sudden lift of the head, a kind of internal listening and in her eyes a fleeting terror, a sort of blankness, like the transoms of doorways, reflecting pure white light. What is she thinking at these moments? Is she imagining his death and life alone?

"It's so warm I could almost go swimming. If I weren't so fat I would."

She is back like a guilty kid, with chocolate crumbs at one corner of her mouth. She sits down on the chaise and swings her bare feet up, lights a cigarette and sighs.

"Go ahead if you want to, nobody can see. That's why I had the fence put up."

"It's been years since I even owned a bathing suit. I guess the biggest trauma is trying them on in the stores. There's always some little salesgirl fluttering around who's twenty-two years old and weighs a hundred and ten. Did you have the pool put in or was it here?"

"It was here but it'd just been put in when I bought the house."

"You mean they put in the pool and sold?"

"They put in the pool and got a divorce."

"Oh dear. Poor gal."

"Poor nothing. She was married to a jerk. She's happier now than she's been for years. The divorce cured her spastic colon."

"Strange, isn't it? When we were kids nobody got divorced. Now it's the national pastime."

"When we were kids, people stayed together and hated it."

"Did you feel that? I didn't. I just felt life was more . . . secure."

"Maybe it was, in some ways. Life in prison has a sort of security."

She smiles and shakes her head. "You really hated being married, didn't you."

"I enjoyed both of my divorces."

"But you didn't have children."

"No, I didn't." I pick up the Book Review section and settle back. She is silent and puts out her cigarette. I try to read, but my mind, irritable today, dwells on Carrie's life. Ellerton,

New Jersey, must be a lot like Summerville, New Jersey. I can see the pleasant tree-lined streets and the bustling modern high school full of athletic equipment instead of books; the pretty wooden Victorian railroad station, where, I bet, Ellerton ladies plant petunias in the window boxes; the small, rather expensive shops full of antiques, fancy cooking gadgets, needlepoint. God, how I'd hate Carrie's life. She lives in an eight-bedroom Victorian house with four kids and no cleaning help, and no doubt, like most of the Summerville ladies, she's an earnest volunteer, drives in three car pools and is on the tennis doubles ladder at the Club. A lot of these ladies come in to see me at the office. They don't know what's wrong, they have all these headaches, they're tired all the time, they get depressed. I can't really tell them what's wrong —it wouldn't help—but I call it the Cream Puff Syndrome, the puffing up of trivia: car pools, tennis matches, and who to get to fix the toilet, into a way of life that has at its center— nothing. There is, on page four of the Book Review, a faded famous picture of Mina. It's the snapshot I took of her in cap and gown, the day we graduated from Smith.

"Dammit."

"What's the matter?"

"Here's another book about Mina. It's by this nut who used to live next to me in the dorm. She was a psychology major. " '*Born to Die*,' it says here, 'is an in-depth analysis of the life of dead poet Mina Van Duyne . . .' How do you like that? Marge hardly knew her . . . 'and the events that led to her tragic suicide at twenty-nine. Miss Knutson puts particular emphasis on the accident that occurred when Miss Van Duyne . . .' Here. Do you want to read this?"

"No."

"There's a note here that says they're bringing out another collection of Mina's poems."

"I never much cared for her poetry."

"Didn't you?"

"No. I thought she was . . . strident."

"I liked that about her. It takes guts to be angry."

"Does it? Well, I don't know. I never understood what she was angry about."

I think of Mina's last letter to me and I say, "She had such a hard time, Carrie."

"I know, I know," Carrie says. "Because of her leg and the accident. But even before that, she was always so—I don't know—dissatisfied. She never would settle for a normal life."

"By normal, you mean married?"

"All right, yes, I do. But isn't marriage for the protection of children? I just can't forget what happened to that child. If she'd married whoever it was, things might have been different."

I don't know what to say. Who can argue with self-righteousness? I am tempted to say, right now, "Carrie, in the wreckage of your husband's car they found the twenty-two-year-old body of—" No, this will not do. Since she leads the perfect life and is one of the happiest housewives on earth, telling her is going to be difficult. Christ, she's so smug she may not even believe me. God's in his heaven, all's right with Ellerton.

A bird flies over our heads and its dark shadow, much magnified, skims the leaf-strewn surface of the pool. The lace vine is in bloom, white masses of flowers cascade over the fence. My little garden of asters and marigolds rehearses the orange and reds of coming fall. I have always liked September, the year's middle age, a sort of beginning, a sort of end. Carrie's eyes glance at me, then away.

TWO

1.

The first time Nell saw Mina was the summer between the fifth and sixth grades at the Horace Van Duyne Memorial Playground. Nell had been swinging, pumping higher and higher and wishing she were brave enough to go over the bars or at least stand up on the swing and pump. She was a fat kid with rosy skin and brown hair who read a lot and had no physical courage. Jimmy Dugan, her special tormentor, followed her everywhere yelling, "Hey, Crisco Kid! Hey! Fat-in-the-can!" Nell wanted to do all sorts of brave daring things but had no heart. In the winter when other kids belly-flopped on their sleds down Suicide Hill, she would wait until they were almost at the bottom, settle herself carefully and shove off, arriving sedately at the foot of the hill when the others were back up at the top again. She was always "it" when they played tag, she was always last in any race. Her mind moved liked lightning; her body, a cumbersome thing she did not understand, lagged behind.

Sliding off the swing, she tweaked at her shorts—they were too tight and always got stuck in the cleft—and went to the water fountain. There was Jimmy Dugan, grinning at her. "Hey, Crisco! Hot enough for ya? I bet this'll melt some of that lard! Hee-hee-hee!" And he stuck his finger into the bubbling jet and shot a silver stream of water at her. She couldn't think of anything to say, but daydreamed of revenge: arsenic instead of sprinkles on his ice cream cone? She watched him run off to the monkey bars, swing himself up and walk on the treacherous top as nonchalant as if he were buoyed by water.

"Hey, fatso, watch this. I'll bet you can't do this!"

He seemed to fall straight down, caught a bar as he passed it, pulled himself up, over and around it. She blinked and in that second a girl appeared at the top of the bars, a thin tanned girl with two long blond braids and white-framed black sunglasses. The girl wore yellow shorts and a yellow and white striped jersey and stepped right over Jimmy as if he didn't exist. She walked on the horizontal bars as if she were a high steelworker, suddenly slid down, caught a bar by her knees, swung under and up. One suntanned knee was criss-crossed by two dirty Band-Aids. Her sunglasses did not fall off. Jimmy had disappeared and the girl was alone on the bars. She did hand catches and knee catches, under and up, over and down, somersaults, and then dropped to the ground, raising a small cloud of ocher dust, and wiped her hands on her shorts. From behind the "rec" house a girl's voice called, "Miii-naaa," and the girl ran off in that direction. She wore boys' basketball sneakers without socks. One of her braids was tied with a yellow ribbon, the other was not.

Susie Dugan, terrible Jimmy's twin sister, was sitting at the edge of the swimming pool. Susie was as red-haired and freckled as Jimmy, but she was nice whereas Jimmy was a brat, and Susie's eyes were kind and brown whereas Jimmy's were sharp and cruel and blue. Susie wore her straight red hair parted in the middle and clipped back on each side of her freckled full moon face with a pink plastic bow barette. The Dugans lived downtown, next to the mills, and had come all the way up the hill for a swim meet. Nell was glad to see Susie. This was Nell's first day at the Horace Van Duyne Playground.

"You gonna be in the swim meet?" Susie asked as Nell sat down next to her.

"Naw," Nell said, sticking her feet into the chlorine-blue

water. She loved to swim, but any kind of competition scared her. If only she could swim all alone, with no one watching. "Are you?"

"Uh-huh. I bet I beat that stupid old Marie Withers. She can't swim a lick and she's so stuck up."

"Hey, Susie?"

"Yeah?"

"Do you know a girl named Mina?"

"Mina? What kind of stupid name is that? Mina who?"

"I don't know her last name."

"Gee, that's a big help. What school does she go to?"

"I don't know."

"Where'd you see her?"

"Over on the monkey bars."

"Oh yeah? Maybe she's a new kid, but who would move to this dumb town?"

"You mean Mina Van Duyne?" Marie Withers said this standing right behind Nell and giving her, as she turned, a terrific view of her long skinny white legs. "I know her. We play together quite often. They live in that big house at the very top of Hill Street." Marie was a terrible snob and had a way of keeping her sharp little chin tilted upward so that you wanted to pinch it. She had sharp little features and her mother bought all her clothes in Albany.

"How come I've never seen her before?" Susie said suspiciously.

"They go away in the summer, you know," Marie said, "to the Cape."

"The Cape?" Nell said. "Where's that?"

"Oh my word," Marie said. "Haven't you ever been to Cape Cod? Oh, it's so divine. I simply adore the Cape."

"I simply adore the Cape," Susie said, and crossed her brown eyes, making Nell laugh.

"Really, I feel so sorry for you, Susie Dugan, you're just so envious of other people. I guess it's not your fault that your father's an alcoholic. I guess if my father were dead-drunk

and out of work most of the time I'd be obnoxious, too."
Marie walked off, her long white legs scissoring along, her
square body in a pink and white ruffled gingham suit looking
like a gift-wrapped box scrunched on top of her legs.

"You know what?" Nell said to Susie. "She looks just like a
stork. I bet she forgets herself and stands on one leg when
nobody's watching."

"Bitch," Susie said. "Rotten bitch. That freak better watch
out. If I ever catch her alone, I'm gonna bash her face in."
And Susie jumped up and, jerking her towel along behind
her, walked off toward the girls' dressing room.

Just the day before, Nell's family had moved from a large
brick Victorian house downtown to a smaller Victorian frame
house on Upper Hill Street. Nicer neighborhood, her mother
had said, explaining the move to Nell. Nell knew that wasn't
the reason. Margarete Dreher loved houses, and the older and
more dilapidated the house, the better she liked it. Driving
through the countryside on a Sunday afternoon, she would
put her hand on her husband's arm and say, "Stop, Hans,
stop. Just look at that place." There, abandoned at the side
of some desolate by-road would be a slant-roofed, tumble-
down, vine-covered wreck that only Mrs. Dreher could love,
and they would stop and she would gaze at it mournfully, and
look back at it longingly as they drove away. She was happiest
when directing workmen, her white hair under a bandana
(she had gone white all at once the year she was thirty-one),
her face pink, standing in the middle of a room full of new
lumber and old plaster. "Over there, we must enlarge that
window, and of course, this wall should come out, if it is possible."

It was a sort of hobby, her buying old houses. But once the
old walls were down and the new windows in and the whole
place was painted and papered from top to bottom, she
would find fault with the house that she had sworn was exactly the home she'd been looking for all her life. A familiar

secret bustle would begin, Mrs. Dreher would acquire a happy, excited look and Mrs. Findlay, a bosomy blonde with diamond-rimmed glasses, red nails and clanking jewelry would come by in her car to take Mrs. Dreher on real estate expeditions. Veddersburg, a dilapidated textile mill town that had never recovered from the depression of the 1930's, offered Mrs. Dreher endless possibilities.

"The bedrooms are just too small," Mrs. Dreher had complained about their first house in Veddersburg. It was on Van Dam Lane, near the river, and Mrs. Dreher had bought it from Joe Smith, the negro Presbyterian Church sexton, for a thousand dollars. The house, a tiny two-hundred-year-old Dutch cottage, had blue and white tiles around the fireplace in the small living room, and the glass in the windowpanes had a marvelous flawed quality, rainbowed wavers and bubbles that kept Nell amused on days when, wrapped in a thick sweater and a blanket and propped on two pillows, she lay on the window seat, too sick to go to kindergarten. A very steep narrow staircase led to the second floor and tiny slant-ceilinged rooms. The Drehers were the only white family to live on Van Dam Lane, but after Mrs. Dreher had had the weathered shingles stained and the shutters painted a dark red and had planted a garden of tulips and daffodils just inside the white picket fence, a delegation of elderly ladies in straw hats, silk print dresses, pearls and white gloves had come to the house to see it, trailing, as they went through the tiny downstairs, waves of lily of the valley perfume.

"Who are they, Mama?" Nell asked.

"The Veddersburg Historical Society," Mrs. Dreher said with a sly smile. She sold the house for eight thousand dollars and they moved to a broken-down farmhouse at the edge of town. After the farmhouse was done over they moved to a large thirty-room Victorian mansion surrounded by a wrought-iron fence which Mrs. Dreher later sold to an undertaker.

Dr. Dreher hated to move and so, with each move, Mrs.

Dreher prepared the way carefully, picking him up practically *in toto* with his bookcases, files, large battered desk, antique black German typewriter, as gently and swiftly as she picked up one of her porcelain pieces, setting him down again in yet another "study" that as much as possible resembled the last one. Orientation was very important to Dr. Dreher. He liked his desk at a window but turned inward. His bookcases had to be at his right hand and his gunmetal gray files lined up at his left hand. The wallpaper pattern Mrs. Dreher used in his study was always the same, alternating stripes of brown and gold, and draperies (very imporant—Dr. Dreher kept them pulled whenever he was thinking) were heavy brown velvet. When Nell first heard the phrase "brown study" she thought instantly of her father's study with its brown light, the golden glow from his lamp, the yellowish brown smoke of his cigarettes, and she supposed that all "studies" were brown. Sometimes, when they had been in a new house for just a few weeks, Dr. Dreher would absent-mindedly drive to the last place and, not really noticing much different, walk in, heading right for his study. One middle of the night, he surprised the young Emersons, who had bought the farmhouse and liked to make love in front of the fieldstone fireplace, and another night, a policeman tried to arrest him for breaking and entering the George L. Medows Funeral Home. Nell, too, hated to move. The torments, each time, of a new school, a new playground! Mrs. Dreher, who calmly assumed, European-style, that Nell would survive as long as she had her family, and never worried about American inventions like playmates, had suddenly mysteriously decided to move into a real neighborhood, where people had yards and lawns and dogs and bicycles and children. Though Nell knew it wasn't that, at all. Mrs. Dreher had simply fallen in love with the old house that had had absolutely nothing done to it for fifty years.

Nell sat on a swing, legs dangling, sucking the last of the orange flavor out of a wooden Popsicle stick. Susie had gone home. The dusty playground was almost empty. A kid came by, but it was only Potty Gorshak, with his huge flop ears and twisted anxious face and crazy staggering walk. A lost soul, her mother called him, and Nell looked the other way as he went muttering by. And then the two girls came out of the "rec" house, Mina and her friend, a tall girl with a pale square face and silver-colored braids. In its dark vault, Nell's heart slipped she wanted so badly to talk to the girls, but as they came up to her she frowned and ducked her head and kicked at the dirt with her shoe. Why couldn't she wear sneakers, she always had to wear these dumb *shoes*.

"Hey," Mina said, standing right in front of her, "aren't you that Susie Dugan's friend? She's a terrific swimmer, she's really good. What's your name? Do you live around here? You're not a bad swimmer, either. Is it hard to do a back dive?"

By five o'clock in the afternoon, when the summer sky had absorbed so much heat and color that it hung over the hill like a ripe golden peach, the three girls walked arm in arm up MacDonald Avenue.

"You're just going to love it up here," Carrie Pettigrew said. "This is the best part of town. All the neatest kids live up here." Her bright blue eyes were so earnest. Small apricot-colored freckles dotted her pale skin.

"Listen," Mina said firmly to Nell at the corner, "tomorrow we'll take you swimming at the Club, okay?"

"What club?" Nell said.

"Our Club," Mina said. "Carrie, you'd better go home now or your mother'll get mad again. We don't want to get her mad, do we?"

"No," Carrie said, and a look of dejection came and went on her face. She ran across the street and they waved at her before she turned away.

"Gee, she's nice," Nell said.

"Yeah," Mina said, and then looking at Nell, she took off her sunglasses, folded them and stuck them in the back pocket of her shorts. She had long rather narrow green eyes under dark, even brows. "Her mother fools around."

Nell tilted her head and looked at Mina curiously. What did she mean?

"You know," Mina said, smiling, but watching Nell all the while. "She f-u-c-k-s other men."

Nell felt a horrid blush come up from the neck of her jersey.

"Oh, it's sad but true," Mina said, tossing back her braids. "I heard my grandmother tell my mother. "But we can't all be perfect, can we? Listen, my dear, don't tell Carrie, okay? Because, you know, we wouldn't want to hurt her. I've got a great idea. Why don't you come to my house for supper? We'll cook hot dogs outside on the barbecue. My mother lets me do that a lot. You're going to love my mom. Everybody does."

Long after it was dark and the fireflies were out, Dr. Van Duyne, Mina's father, drove Nell home in his long gray Packard with the swan on the hood. The Drehers' new house was dark and spooky and still unsettled. Nell walked through it carefully, not knowing where the light switches were and bumping into pieces of furniture. She ran down the back porch steps toward the orange dot of her mother's cigarette and told her about Mina and Carrie and the Van Duyne house, a huge house full of kids—so many kids you couldn't really sort out the Van Duynes' from the others. They had played FBI, all of them, and had cooked hot dogs on the brick barbecue and had a whole watermelon for dessert, and Mina and Carrie and Nell were friends.

Nell's mother smiled. "You see," she said, "I told you you would make new friends."

It was a soft navy blue June night dotted here and there with the lime green lights of fireflies. Her mother sat back in the old canvas beach chair and sighed. A marvelous smell of roses drifted toward them.

"You know her mother, don't you? Mrs. Van Duyne?"

"Of course," her mother said. Even in the dark Nell could tell that she was smiling. "She's head of the Ladies' Medical Auxiliary—Dr. Van Duyne's a surgeon—and last year she was president of the Tuesday Night Club. She's very nice."

"And do you know Carrie's mother, too?"

"Oh yes," her mother said, but the smile in her voice faded. "She is . . . very beautiful."

"Carrie's so nice."

"I'm glad."

"Is Mrs. Van Duyne a friend of Mrs. Withers?"

"Mrs. Withers? I don't know. Why do you ask?"

"You don't like Mrs. Withers, do you?"

"I don't dislike Mrs. Withers. She is only a little . . . narrow."

"Narrow?"

"Sometimes when a person is born and grows up and lives in one small place, she or he thinks that place is the only one in the world, and that is called being narrow."

"Isn't she the lady you had the fight with, about that painting?"

"My, my, what a memory! Yes, but it wasn't a fight, it was only a discussion. Unfortunately, Mrs. Whizzers—"

"Withers—" Nell said, automatically correcting her mother.

"Whizzers," Nell's mother said again, trying but failing the terrible American *th* test, "is not very well educated. Just look up at the stars, Nell. Do you see the Little Dipper? What a lovely night!"

In a hole between the leafy maples, the sky appeared deeply black and star-speckled, a patch of rich sequined cloth. The lofty maples sheltered cicadas, but the mosquitoes had not yet arrived in town for the summer. Sitting there looking up, Nell thought how much she loved her mother, the white Victorian house looming behind them, the town, the valley with its broad, slowly winding brown river, the Adirondacks, where they would go next month, and the whole black star-sprinkled world that was so calm and lovely tonight. If only nothing would ever change. If only there was not this little nubbin of worry.

"Ah," Nell's mother said, expressing it, "I wonder where your father is. I hope he didn't get lost again on the Parksville Road. Lately, I don't know—he's so tired and depressed. He forgets where he is. Tell me, isn't it time for you to go to bed?"

"I can sleep late tomorrow."

"But you will want to get up and play with your friends."

One by one, the lights in the house next door went out. A little breeze brought them the silver tinkle of wind chimes from their neighbor's porch.

"Dear God," Mrs. Dreher said, "I'm so tired. Come. It's already late."

At the kitchen door, Nell stopped for a moment before she went in and looked out at the yard, its dark shapes and shrubs not yet familiar. She heard the sound of a tired car—her father's—coming up the hill, and she sighed. Everything was all right. Headlights lit up the back drive. He was home. This was home. Everything was all right, and perhaps they would never move again.

"So this is the famous Nell Dreher," Mr. Pettigrew said, sitting down at the table, "the one who does the back dive."

That morning Mina had left for the Cape and Carrie had asked Nell for dinner and overnight. Awed, Nell had accepted. The Pettigrews were having Eunice fried chicken and baking powder biscuits. In her ignorance, Nell had thought that Eunice was a geographic area—like Southern, or Maryland, but Eunice was Mrs. Pettigrew's housekeeper. It wasn't even Sunday, only Thursday night, and there were flowers and lit candles on the table and Mr. and Mrs. Pettigrew had had drinks before dinner on the terrace. Although it was eighty-five degrees, Mr. Pettigrew put on his seersucker sports coat before sitting down to eat.

"A back dive is real easy," Nell said. "Carrie can do one already."

"Carrie's built just like a boy," Mrs. Pettigrew said. "I'm sure she can do all those athletic things."

"Not all boys are good athletes," Mr. Pettigrew said. "I was never much of an athlete."

"That's right," Mrs. Pettigrew said coldly, "you weren't." She had on a black halter and a white skirt and sat smoking Kools through the whole meal. Whenever she moved her hands, her silver bangles jingled, a pretty delicate sound.

"You're a good golfer, Daddy," Carrie said loyally. "Everyone says so."

"Carrie, will you please not pick up the chicken at the dining room table?" said Mrs. Pettigrew, and Nell, hoping no one had noticed, put her chicken leg back on the plate.

"Cynthia," Mr. Pettigrew said, "come on, kiddo, relax. It's summer."

"Her table manners are terrible," Mrs. Pettigrew said indifferently, and put her cigarette out in a silver ashtray shaped like a clamshell. "At least she's not an imbecile. I was in Jordan's yesterday and I heard the most awful racket outside. That crazy Gorshak boy had walked right out in front of a car on Main Street. Lord knows why it hasn't happened before this, the way he wanders everywhere and the crazy way he walks. He should have been institutionalized years ago."

"My God," Mr. Pettigrew said. "Was he badly hurt?"

Mrs. Pettigrew shrugged. "No, the car missed him and he ran off. You wonder why they didn't drown him at birth."

"Don't talk that way," Mr. Pettigrew said to her sharply, and then turned to Carrie with a smile and asked if her friend Mina had gotten off to the Cape.

"Uh-huh," said Carrie.

("Not 'uh-huh,'" said Mrs. Pettigrew, "and not 'yeah.' The word is 'yes.'")

"Yes," Carrie said, "and we didn't get started on our tree house, either."

"Aha," Mr. Pettigrew said, "a tree house. Where is this famous tree house going to be?"

Nell and Carrie glanced at each other and smiled. "We can't tell," Carrie said. "It's a secret place. It was Mrs. Van Duyne's idea. She used to have a tree house when she was little."

"Rhee in a tree house," Mrs. Pettigrew said. "There's a charming picture."

"Don't pick on my friend Rhee," Mr. Pettigrew said to his wife.

"I wouldn't dream of picking on Rhee Van Duyne," Mrs. Pettigrew said. "I adore Rhee, everyone does. She's the perfect wife and mother."

"Maybe Charles is the perfect husband," Mr. Pettigrew said blandly.

"Carrie," Mrs. Pettigrew said, "if you eat one more biscuit you will grow up to be a big fat slob and no one will take you out on dates. Next week, Judson, as soon as I get the pumpkin here off to camp, I'm going down to New York City."

"All righty," Mr. Pettigrew said, and buttered another biscuit. He was the only one at the table who had picked up his chicken leg in his fingers. "Going to stay with Elaine and George, are you?"

"They'll be away. George has to go to California on business. Elaine says I can use the apartment."

"That works out perfectly, then," Mr. Pettigrew said. "The convenience of it."

"Would you rather I stayed at a hotel?"

"Why on earth would I? This will be simply perfect for you, dear."

"I could stay home, dear, is that what you want?"

"I want what you want, dear."

"Daddy, why can't I ever go to the Cape with Mina? She's asked me three years in a row."

"Because you're going to camp, sweetie."

"Couldn't I go to the Cape just for a week?"

"And miss the big Pow Wow and the annual All-Star Softball Game?"

"I wouldn't mind going to the Cape," Mrs. Pettigrew said. "God, another August at Crystal Lake with the flies and mosquitoes and the rowboat and Saturday nights playing bridge with the Simpsons. You'd think that just once we could go someplace different, someplace not in those creepy dark mountains, someplace your grandfather didn't build with his own two hands."

"Nell's going to be at Blueberry Lake in August, aren't you Nell?" said Carrie. "That's not far away. Maybe we could see each other. Wouldn't that be fun?"

"Yeah . . . *es*," said Nell.

"Clear the table, Carrie dear, will you?" said Mrs. Pettigrew, and lit another cigarette. She got up from the table as if terribly tired and went into the living room, where she stood at the French doors that led out to the terrace. Nell thought how beautiful she looked standing there, so beautiful and fragile and sad.

"Oh Christ, Judson," Mrs. Pettigrew said, "will you look at that? The Johnsons' St. Bernard has crapped on our terrace again."

Everyone in Veddersburg, New York, knew that Carrie Pettigrew's mother was a real beauty, just as Carrie knew, that she, Carrie, was not. Nell admired Mrs. Pettigrew terrifically. She always looked as if she'd just come from some elegant exciting place and was going on to another. She was very slender and held her dark beautifully shaped head high up on her long neck, as if presenting you with a rare flower. Her dark hair was cut short and parted in the middle like the Duchess of Windsor's, and she had dark brown eyes, evenly arched dark eyebrows and dead-white skin. She bought her clothes in New York City and she never wore "housedresses." But at the corner of her mouth there was a little dimple of dissatisfaction and in her dark eyes there was a cold bleak light. Coming out of church on a Sunday morning, you could see the old ladies' heads bobbing together—each hat a nest of straw and veiling and fake red cherries. What were they saying? You bent your head forward to hear. "Spoiled," they whispered. "Poor Judson Pettigrew. Spoiled, spoiled, spoiled." Down the street, Mrs. Pettigrew slid behind the wheel of her very own little red car—a tiny gay MG—and the other ladies, standing there on the church steps in their dowdy silk print dresses and gloves and pearls and straw hats, had to wait for their husbands to bring around dusty Fords and good old dependable Chevies, and said to themselves, "Spoiled," while Cynthia Pettigrew, one slender elegantly I. Miller-shod foot hard on the gas pedal, zoomed away, Carrie slowly waving her hand at you out of the rolled-down window.

She had everything. She had a car of her own to drive, and lots of beautiful clothes, and a membership in the Roaring Brook Country Club. In the middle of the depression, when young couples in Veddersburg had to move in with their parents because jobs were so scarce, Jud Pettigrew built his young wife a beautiful house in the New England clapboard style, with dark green shutters and four bathrooms. He was "handy," Mr. Pettigrew was, and if you dropped by Carrie's house on a weekend, you would hear him in some far-off corner of the house, sawing and whistling. Just lately, he had taken off the whole back wall of the living room and put in folding French doors that led out to the flagstone terrace he had put in himself. The Pettigrew kitchen was a gleaming stainless steel procession of immaculate equipment and the rooms of the house were papered and curtained and chintz-covered by a decorating firm from New York City.

Judson Pettigrew was a lawyer and according to Mina had only three faults: he bit his nails, he had a high offensive laugh like the whinny of a horse and Sundays, if you sat in back of him at church, you longed to lean forward and brush the dandruff from his navy blue serge shoulders. He was a tall lean man with a long handsome face and thinning sandy-colored hair. He laughed a lot. If Mrs. Pettigrew made one of her stinging cold remarks, he simply laughed, throwing back his head so that you plainly saw his bristly Adam's apple. He was good to Carrie and took the girls to baseball games, to the circus when it arrived in June, and to the County Fair in September. But there was something wrong at the Pettigrews' and you didn't like going there. Eunice O'Brian, the house-keeper, was getting old and she didn't like kids around mess-ing up, and she yelled a lot. And if Mrs. Pettigrew was home you didn't know whether she'd get mad over nothing, the way she did, or if maybe she'd come in and sit on Carrie's bed, looking sad and pathetic, and want to talk when you didn't have anything in particular you wanted to say to her. You wondered why Mrs. Pettigrew was so unhappy. Although she'd been born and brought up just twenty miles down the river she wasn't comfortable with Veddersburg, was more alien to it than Mrs. Dreher, who'd been raised thousands of miles away. People said she gave herself airs. Mrs. Dreher said sharply that she made her own loneliness. If only, occasionally, she would smile. She never smiled. Not once in all the years Nell knew her did she remember Cynthia Pettigrew smiling.

The first night that Nell slept at Carrie's she was awakened by a noise. There was a moon and a white light came in through the dotted swiss curtains. Nell got up to look out the window. Down below on the terrace she saw Mr. Pettigrew in pajamas and bathrobe. He was squatting, scraping at something with a trowel. He tossed the stuff into the bushes, stuck the trowel into a flower bed and sat down in a wrought-iron chair. He took a drink from the table and sat looking up at the moon, sipping his drink. She could hear the ice clink in the glass, could see his rumpled moonlit hair and the bald spot on the back of his head, and every once in a while she heard him make a peculiar noise in his throat like a cough or a hiccough or a sigh.

"Uh-oh," Mina said, and moved back into the shadowy woods.

"What?" Carrie said. They had spent a long day swimming at the Roaring Brook Country Club, had walked slowly home across the golf course, crossed the highway, taken the shortcut through Crazy Bob's farm and come home the back way, through the wooded bird sanctuary which ended at a white pine tree that began the Van Duynes' back yard. At the other end of the yard they could see thirteen-year-old Clay, in blue jeans but shirtless, cutting the grass with stoical evenness. Above the steady sputtering of the hand motor, a booming voice came through the small screened windows of the Van Duynes' kitchen. A new pale blue Lincoln was parked in the driveway just in front of the barn.

"Christaforio," Mina said, "I forgot. I was supposed to go out to lunch with my grandmother."

"You shouldn't swear," Carrie said. "Besides, I'll bet you forgot on purpose."

"Listen to that," Mina said cheerfully. "I bet she's giving my mother the business on what a rotten kid I am. You should have heard her last night, on Julia."

"What'd Julia do?" Nell asked. "Did she flunk out?"

"Naw," Mina said. "It's worse than that. I'll tell you later. Hey. Maybe we could sneak into the barn and go up to the loft."

"Clay'll see us, won't he?" Nell said.

"Not if we go back through the woods and around."

"I hate that loft," Carrie said. "It's filthy and makes me sneeze, and it's full of cobwebs and bugs."

"Gee whiz, Carrie," Mina complained, "sometimes you're such a chicken-dope."

The noise of the mower stopped. Clay mopped his face with a bandana, then looked at an upstairs window and yelled "Buzz! Hey, Buzz, get off the stupid phone. It's your turn." Clay left the mower parked in the middle of the grass next to a striped croquet stick and walked off toward the barn. The screen door squawked and slammed. Buzz came out, stood on the shady porch, looked at the mower, yawned and not so much moved as drifted toward it. He was sixteen, tall, lean and tennis-tanned, with perfectly combed dark hair and amazing blue eyes. He wore white tennis shorts, no shirt and tennis sneakers. He stood looking down at the mower for a minute, then grabbed the handles violently and ran, as if attacking the grass. At the end of this first row he stopped and lit a cigarette.

Again, the screen door slammed. A very tall, heavy woman came out. Her piled-up mass of blue-white hair was just shades lighter than her linen dress. Her white high heels seemed to pierce to the very heart the quivering old porch floorboards.

"Good-bye, dear," the woman called to Buzz. "Don't forget to call on the Dunbars when you get to the Cape."

"Okay, Grandma," Buzz said. "Thanks. Have a nice trip."

"Honest-to-God," Mina said, her mouth moving sarcastically sideways. "He's such a brown-nose. He'd never get into Harvard all by himself, he's got to brown-nose his way in. She keeps finding all these contacts for him. It's disgusting. He's such a jerk."

"Why is he a jerk?" Nell asked. She thought Buzz was very handsome. Clay was funny and nice, but Buzz made her feel strange—shy and wriggly at the same time.

"He just is," Mina said. "Don't ask me why, he was born that way."

The pale blue Lincoln backed out of the drive in a zigzag pattern, spewing up waves of gravel. Clay came out of the barn. The girls walked out of the woods.

"Where've you been, punk?" Clay said, reaching for one of Mina's braids and pulling it. He was still red-faced from mowing, his face, chest and arms covered with sweat and bits of grass. Nell saw there was curly light brown hair in his armpits and politely looked the other way. "You're gonna get it, you know. She was really mad. She was gonna buy you some clothes, idiot."

"I don't care," Mina said. "She only buys the stuff that she likes. Why don't you go take a shower? You're all sweaty and disgusting. And what were you doing in the barn, smoking? I'll bet you were, weren't you?"

"Go soak your head, will ya? And don't think you're getting out of the grass this time. See that other croquet stake? You've got to do from there on down."

"Aw, shut up, garbage can man."

"No, you, piss-face."

"Mina?" Mrs. Van Duyne said, a bulky shape behind the screen door. "Is that you? Will you come in here, please? Oh, hello, girls. Mina, I'll talk to you later. Do you realize how rude you were to your grandmother?"

Later it seemed to Nell that the Van Duyne house was really two different houses. There were the places she knew so well: the back yard with its swing and hammock and clumps of bushes for hiding; the barn, smelling of gasoline, with its dimlit cobwebby rafters and sudden flap of scissor-tailed swallows; Mina's room—neat, bare, cold, with a little white-painted roll-top desk and always a pile of library books on the windowsill tangled up with the organdy curtains, and most of all, the kitchen. The kitchen was in a little wooden wing that had been built onto the house at right angles. It was shabby and sunny, with yellow walls and dull blue linoleum that needed to be replaced. Everything in the Van Duynes' kitchen needed to be replaced. The white porcelain sink was chipped and gouged, the gas stove was a boxy-hipped model that stood on four pointed toes and the refrigerator wore its old humming motor on the top of its head. To the left of the kitchen door was a round wooden table which held a ceaseless flow of school books, library books, Book-of-the-Month Club books, mail, homework papers, jars full of grass blades and insects, sticky jam pots. The kitchen was always full of activity, and in strange contrast, the other rooms of the house—and there were many—seemed cold and mysterious. There was the formal, wainscotted dining room with a soot-darkened portrait of sly-eyed Jacobus Van Duyne, "The Ancestor," on one wall. Then you crossed the long hall with its fanlit doors at either end and there was the living room with its gray ceilings and draperies and its leprous patchy walls and its heavy mahogany furniture and its odor of dust and dead ashes from the fireplace. Most remote of all was Dr. and Mrs. Van Duyne's bedroom, a dark room with a fireplace and massive four-poster bed and a large wardrobe with mirrored doors that lazily reflected nothing at all but bluish light. Nell loved her mother's bedroom. There was always a lingering scent of face powder and cologne, and on the dressing table, intriguing grown-up things: a gold bracelet, bits of veiling, a glove with a pearl button at the wrist. The Van Duynes' bedroom was severe, gave no hints or clues, and in fact, if you left the kitchen, you felt uneasy, as if you were a guest, not of the family but of some sort of secret society, where the rules were strict but unknown and where you could never, never, no matter how much you might want to, join, or even find out the rules.

Later, there were questions Nell wanted to ask. Why was it that Mrs. Van Duyne sewed, cooked, ironed, baked and even read in the kitchen? Why was it that when she brought in flowers from her beautiful garden she put them all in the kitchen? Carrie said Mrs. Van Duyne sat in the kitchen so that you'd always know where to find her. And indeed, she did seem like the center of a huge unseen web and everything in the household seemed to flow from her, come back to her.

Today she had on a faded blue cotton dress, torn out under one arm. Her arms were full of clean laundry. Open suitcases stood gap-jawed all around the kitchen floor. She put the laundry on the kitchen table and began folding it and placing it in piles.

"Peter," she said to herself, "Buzz, Clay, Mina," dealing out the folded T-shirts as if they were cards. "Watch those suitcases, girls. Clay, Peter, Peter, Buzz."

"We're going downstairs, Ma."

"Where?"

"Down to the cellar. It's nice and cool down there, and Clay and Peter won't bother us."

Mrs. Van Duyne laughed. She was a tall woman, heavy in the body, with a large handsome nose and pale kind eyes and a mass of brown and silver-streaked hair that she wore loosely pinned up into a knot at the top of her head. If you stayed in the kitchen with her any length of time you would hear an occasional ping like the striking of a far-off bell, and she would vaguely lift one hand to her hair and secure the remaining pins. She looked at Mina proudly and said, "What a funny girl you are. Always full of ideas."

They didn't turn on the light but sat on three orange crates near Quasimodo, the huge hump-backed furnace. The cool cellar smelled of damp dirt, and through the canted window, propped open on an old Mason jar, they could hear the uneven rhythm of Buzz's mowing and smell the cut grass. Upstairs, over their heads, Mrs. Van Duyne moved around the kitchen, and through a pipe overhead they heard the surge of water moving downward from the third floor, where Clay was taking a shower.

"Now tell us," Carrie said.

"Tell you what?" Mina said, teasing.

"You know," Carrie said. "About Julia."

"Did she flunk out?" Nell asked. Wasn't that the worst thing that could happen to anyone? She had once asked her father what original sin meant and he'd said, lowering his newspaper, "Ignorance." Across the room, her mother had laughed.

"Okay, I'll tell you, but promise not to tell anyone, not your mother, or your father, or any of the kids . . ."

"Okay, okay," Nell said.

"Do you promise, Carrie?" Mina said.

"I promise, Mina, for goodness' sake."

"Well, then," Mina said, and sat up straight, "she eloped."

"Oh!" Carrie said.

"So what?" Nell said.

"Isn't that a riot?" Mina said.

Carrie said primly, "I don't think that's funny, Mina, I think that's sad, not to come home and have a wedding with your family and friends and all. Was it someone nobody liked?"

"I don't know," Mina said, "we haven't met him. My mother cried at first. My grandmother yelled at my mother something terrible. My father was mad about the money. You know? Because she only finished a year and Vassar's expensive."

Dr. Van Duyne frightened Nell. He was a tall, lean, elegant man with silver hair and bristling eyebrows. He seemed cold and stern to Nell, although Mrs. Dreher said he was very handsome. Nell didn't care much for Mina's grandmother, either. Every Sunday morning, seconds before the bell tolled just at eleven, Edwina Van Duyne came down the central aisle of the church trailing perfume and silk and mink, and her thin legs in high heels seemed to Nell like exclamation points, surprised ! ! at the job they were required to do. Not until she was seated and had said her little prayer did the minister give Mr. Augustus Chew the signal, and the little bald organist would pounce upon the keys as if in anger, and only then would the choir, waiting restlessly in the vestibule, start singing, and Mrs. Dreher, standing up for the first hymn, would say to Nell, amused, "God has to wait for Edwina Van Duyne."

"But why did she elope?" Carrie asked.

"I don't know," Mina said. "Julia always was a little nutty."

"Aren't they coming home at all?"

"No, they went right to New York City. They're going to live there. He's a playwright."

"A playwright!" Nell said. "Wow, that's really interesting. What sort of plays does he write?"

"He wrote a play that was almost on Broadway last year, I forget the name of it. He teaches playwriting in New York."

"Gee," Nell said, "I think that sounds exciting, living in New York City and getting to know actors and everything."

"My mother's taken me to New York City twice," Carrie said. "I didn't like it much. It's crowded and dirty and there are all sorts of weird people."

"The worst thing though," Mina said, "is that he's Jewish."

"Oh no," Carrie said. "No wonder she eloped. Wasn't your father really upset? My parents would die if I even married a Catholic. My father gets all upset about the Catholics. He says they all do exactly what the priests tell them, even how to vote and everything. Gosh, if I married somebody Jewish, they'd commit suicide."

"What's wrong with Jews?" Nell asked curiously. "They don't have priests, do they?"

Carrie and Mina looked at each other and laughed. Mina said, "We could ask Hitler, but he's dead."

"You can ask Julia, if she ever comes home," Carrie said.

"But what's wrong with Jews?" Nell asked again, puzzled. She knew her father was half Jewish and half Catholic but he didn't talk about it much, he had only said once gruffly that all religions were mainly nonsense and that the Catholics with their priests and confessions were as bad as the Jews with their rabbis and rules. Her mother had just shrugged.

"It was dumb of Julia," Mina said. "My father's going down to New York next week and he's not even going to visit them. My mother wanted to go with him but he said, 'under no condition' could she go. You wait, though, my mom will straighten it all out. She's good at things like that. She's always saying there are only good people and bad people, no matter what else they are."

"Your mom is so nice," Carrie said. "I love your mom." She bent her head shyly, so that you could see the pink part in her hair. Poor Carrie. Her mother pulled her hair into braids so tight you could always see her tender scalp. "My mom's going to New York next week, too."

"Oh, she's always going to New York," Mina said rudely. "How come she goes to New York so much of the time?"

"I don't know," Carrie said.

"I think it's dumb," Mina said, and jumped up. "Why would anyone go to New York if he could be at Cape Cod? Let's go see if there's any spice cake left. Do you like spice cake, Nell?"

But a blurry movement caught the corner of Nell's eye and then a flying red arc landed at her feet and suddenly exploded. The girls screamed and drew together, and then a small bony kid wearing glasses and a baseball cap jumped out from behind Quasimodo.

"I heard what you said, Mina!" Peter screamed joyfully. "I heard every word. I'm gonna tell Ma you told. I'm gonna tell Dad, too! Now you're gonna get it! Now you're gonna be in big trouble!"

In the kitchen, Mrs. Van Duyne was ironing. She spread a shirt out on the board and smoothed it with a large red-knuckled hand. She dipped her fingers into a bowl of water and sprinkled the shirt as if giving a blessing, then with even strokes nosed the iron gently into a dart while two plumes of steam rose on either side. The kitchen smelled of fresh ironing, of milk and the spice cake the girls sat eating right out of their cupped hands.

"But he always does that, Mom, he follows us everywhere and spies on us. Aren't you even going to punish him for having firecrackers? Honest-to-God, I think he's a mental, like Potty Gorshak."

"He's just lonesome, Mina," Mrs. Van Duyne said. "There aren't any boys his age around here. Next year when he has a bike he'll be more independent."

"I'll be dead by that time," Mina said, "or insane."

"When I was about your age," Mrs. Van Duyne said, lifting the iron and setting it on its heel, "I built myself a tree house." Carefully, she peeled the shirt off the board and arranged it on a hanger. "We lived on a farm, you know, near Tolson's Mill. We had a good-sized house but I had two older sisters and a younger brother. That was your uncle Phil, Mina, the one who was killed in the war. I suppose I was a strange child—I loved to be by myself and read, but I had the kind of mother that never let you alone. If she saw you just sitting there reading, she'd find something for you to do. There was always a lot to be done, too. It seemed to me I never had any place I could be by myself. One day, I noticed an old apple tree at the very edge of the orchard, almost in the woods. We had some lumber lying around in the barn and I took it little by little and pretty soon I'd hammered together a tree house. Of course, after a while, everyone noticed it but for a few weeks anyway I had a place all my own. It was the only time in my life I've had a place of my own." She smiled and spread another shirt on the ironing board.

Nell said, "We could do that, Mina, you know? Why don't we? We could build a tree house."

Mrs. Van Duyne smiled. "You'll have to hurry. We're leaving for the Cape tomorrow."

Mina said, "We could build it when we get back. We'll make it our clubhouse. We'll pick out a place today and not tell anyone where it is."

Outside, there was the sound of tires spinning in gravel. "Well now," Mrs. Van Duyne said, "here's your grandmother, back again. Mina, don't you leave without telling her . . ."

But Mina was already out the door with Carrie right after her, leaving Nell on the step as the lady arrived. She swept past Nell and into the kitchen.

"Oh, my dear," she said to Mina's mother, "I've just had the worst experience. I'm so upset. Can you reach Charles for me? That awful child, Henrietta, that idiot boy, the one who wanders all over town—he ran right in front of my car down in front of Jordan's. I slammed on the brakes and now the back of my car is ruined. I don't understand it, Henrietta, why is he allowed to wander around this way? My heart, Henrietta, call Charles. And will you call the pharmacy for me? I have the most awful pain . . ."

At the very back of the yard, at the edge of the woods, Mina silently appeared, put a finger to her lips, and, rotating her left arm in a large circle, beckoned to Nell to come.

4.

In the stark white evening light of the freshly painted uncurtained living room, Mrs. Dreher lay on the sofa with her moccasins off and her feet up, looking at old photographs. The photographs were kept in an old yellow box shaped like a pirate's treasure chest. It had once held chocolates, and whenever its ribboned hinges were lifted, a dark sweetish aroma haunted the room.

"Strange," Mrs. Dreher said. "I remember everything we did that day, how we shopped at Tietz's, that we had veal for lunch, that the weather was clear and bright and there was a strong smell of coffee in the street, but I can't remember the color of that hat. Did I ever wear such a thing? What a silly style."

It was a photograph of her mother *en promenade* on the Kurfürstendamm, in a long droopy belted coat and a cloche pulled down to her eyes and on a leash she held her dog, Napoleon, who even in the photograph had a poodle's special alert nervous quiver.

Of all their possessions, this box full of memorabilia, photographs, postcards, letters upon which the ink had long ago turned a rusty violet, seemed to the wandering Drehers the most important. It was a pictorial condensation of four generations of family life, and Nell could remember being very young, three or four, and looking at these photographs with something she would later call a sense of time—an eerie, inconsolable feeling, the sadness of the near past, so close, so utterly unknowable—these people in stiff collars and high hairdos, or short jazz-age dresses or the baggy clothes of the terrible 1930's. Here, for example, in the sepia tones of 1910, was the late blasted house of her mother's family, a large wooden house, very tall and fancifully carved, surrounded by a picket fence, on the very shore of the Baltic Sea, and in front of the gate a tiny group of persons in a blur of white with sunstruck smiles. Then there were pictures of Nell's father, a young German officer in a spiked helmet sitting handsomely on a World War I horse, and later, in a striped bathrobe sitting in a wheelchair. On to Berlin in the twenties: her father in evening dress, her mother in various costumes and disguises—in long black stockings and short harlequin pantaloons and lots of rouge, sitting on a piano, smoking; her parents in ski knickers and heavy turtleneck sweaters standing on a blindingly white mountain—her mother with a knit cap pulled right down to her straight black brows; her father in a bathing suit sitting in a sailboat at sunset, the water almost black, a thin quivering gold line dividing lake and sky and his eyeglasses and metal belt buckle catching the last rays of sunlight. And other pictures of friends and relations Nell had never met, sitting at a picnic table under the speckled shade of a tree, her mother always in the middle of any gathering, smiling radiantly, her light blond hair in a halo of sunlight; pictures of people all unknown to Nell or dead, and places destroyed, her grandparents' house at Peenemunde leveled by a V-2 that failed and her parents' cottage at the lake outside of Berlin broken up for firewood one hard winter after World War II, and the apartment in Berlin long gone, with its "art moderne" furniture and paintings and rows of books.

Photographs followed them into the New World. Snub-nosed Nell at five stuffed into a snowsuit and put upon tiny skis; Nell in a bathing suit sitting on the dock of the cottage they rented in the Adirondacks, the cottage only a glimpse of white behind dark evergreens (and everything, everything came back to Nell with this out-of-focus photograph, the dusty pine smell of the cottage, the aching blue coldness of the lake and the deep-shaded mysterious evergreen forest with its floor of reddish brown needles and quivering shafts of dusty sunlight eerily piercing the shade between silent trees) just as that Berlin street, circa 1929, the smell of coffee, the clang of trolleys, the smoke and cinder taste of city air had come back to Mrs. Dreher.

"Gone," Nell's mother murmured. "Gone forever."

The door of the waiting room tinkled and slammed. "At last," she said, and swung her feet to the floor and into the moccasins. "I thought that woman would never leave. This is just what we need now, Anna Gorshak for your father to deal with." She got up and padded into the kitchen. On the other side of the house, her father's office also opened into the kitchen, and in another moment Nell heard her father's low tired voice. A cabinet door banged, a drawer was jerked open scaring the silverware, water ran in the sink, the frying pan hissed on the stove. Her father said something, wearily.

"Of course," her mother answered in a high angry voice. "Why shouldn't you be tired, that woman was here for an hour and a half. She's crazy, Hans. No other doctor would deal with her." Plates were set down on the table—click, clack. Glancing at Nell, who stood in the kitchen doorway, Mrs. Dreher said to her husabnd, "Ach, *was*, she's a paranoid. You don't have to be a doctor to see this. And do you think she really cares about the boy? She's too sick herself. He runs all over town alone and hungry."

Dr. Dreher sat at the table with his head in his hands. Nell filled a glass with cold water and stood leaning against the sink, drinking it, and her mother, glancing at Nell again, annoyingly continued the conversation in a burst of high-speed German.

In Veddersburg, Upper Hill Street was solidly residential, but halfway down the hill, just at de Groot's Guest and Tourist Home, with its long porch full of wicker rocking chairs and nodding white heads, the street changed. There was Fanny Farmer on one corner and Lefkowitz Fine Home Furnishings at Cut Rate Prices on the other. Next to Fanny Farmer was the old Alhambra Theater and next to the theater the Starlite Billiard Parlour and next to that, Lotus Land Florists ("grave covers our specialty") and in between the pool hall and the florist, a dark smelly doorway, where, Nell remembered, she had often seen Potty Gorshak sitting on the step with his twitching head and his bitter anxious look.

He was always peculiarly dressed. His pants were men's pants cut off at the knees, held up to his armpits by black suspenders. He wore men's shoes but no socks. His mother kept his head shaved, except for a fine fair fuzz, and except for a sailor's pea coat in winter, his clothes even on the coldest days were exactly the same. Jud Pettigrew had his law offices over the Starlite and the Gorshaks lived on the floor above, which was convenient for Mrs. Gorshak since she was a cleaning lady and took care of all the offices in the building. Mr. Gorshak had been dead or gone for so long no one remembered him. Mrs. Gorshak could speak English but didn't much—most of the time, if you saw her somewhere on the street she was muttering, in what language it was hard to tell. She was a thin angular woman with stringy brown hair screwed back into a bun. She always wore a long black coat with a red fox fur collar, and underneath it a variety of dresses with uneven hemlines.

Potty got his name because, in kindergarten, he had raised his hand every five minutes or so and said, "Teacher, I gotta go potty." He stayed in kindergarten until the teacher got sick of seeing him at the back of the room, staring into space, his head nodding, his fingers twiddling—some part of him was always twitching or jerking. He walked in short spastic lurching steps, as if any second he would fall over. He got pushed around a lot and picked on and in class nobody wanted to sit near him, he smelled so bad. Sometimes, if the teacher ignored him too long he wet his pants, and then he would smell terrible, a dank musty odor, and the next day he was sure to come to school with black and blue marks on his arms or a split lip or a swelling the size of an egg on his fuzzy head. Late that afternoon, Nell had come home from Mina's to find Potty sitting on the front porch steps. Just then her mother came out and said sharply, "You go around to the other door. Go on, that's the waiting room door." He looked at her with his troubled face and then got up and walked in his lurching ridiculous gait to the side door of the house and sat down on the steps there.

"I don't know, Hans," Mrs. Dreher said, sitting down at the kitchen table across from her husband. "Isn't there anyone to take care of people like this?"

"What do you suggest?" Dr. Dreher asked mildly, lifting his head. "A nice concentration camp?"

Mrs. Dreher said nothing, only shook her head.

"The boy is ill, you see," Dr. Dreher said.

"I see that," Mrs. Dreher said. "He's ill because she never took care of him, and who knows, perhaps he was born defective. These people always have strange things wrong with them."

"Ah yes," Dr. Dreher said, picking up his fork and letting it drop, "these people" (his tone was ironic) "can't afford meat and oranges, and live on crackers and Coca-Cola. I think the boy can be helped. I have put him on a special diet. First of all, he is very malnourished."

"Of course," said Mrs. Dreher scornfully. "And who is to provide this special diet? You? Even if you gave her the food, do you think she has intelligence enough to cook it? She herself needs care, Hans. Now be careful with her. You shouldn't get so involved. She's not normal."

"Quite correct," Dr. Dreher said. "She is paranoid, she thinks the world is against her. I think she is right: the world *is* against her. Was there mail today?"

"Of course," Mrs. Dreher said. "We always have mail. A

telephone bill, two medical journals, four samples from drug companies."

"Nothing else?"

"Nothing."

"It's been so long since we wrote them. Shouldn't we have some word soon?"

"I don't know, Hans."

"I think," Dr. Dreher said, "if we don't hear from the Red Cross soon, I should go to New York City. I understand there are private agencies there that will help."

"Are you going to New York, too?" Nell said. "Everybody's going to New York. Mrs. Pettigrew's going to New York and Dr. Van Duyne's going to New York."

"What?" Dr. Dreher said, surprised. He hadn't noticed Nell standing there, at the kitchen sink.

Mrs. Dreher's mouth pulled to one side, the way it did when she was going to make a joke, and she said something to Dr. Dreher in rapid German, and then she said, turning her head toward Nell, "Now you must go to bed. Every night it gets later." And then she said something again in German to Dr. Dreher and he smiled sadly and shook his head, and her parents sat smiling sadly at each other across the kitchen table.

THREE

1.

Tuesday. Every fifteen minutes a very starched young nurse with a turned-up nose and a smooth blond bun comes into Kurtz's room to check his vital signs: pulse, respiration, blood pressure, temperature. She adjusts the drip on his IV, then peels back his eyelids and looks at his pupils: enlarged pupils are bad, uneven pupil size very bad. Constriction of the pupils is good, showing some response to light, that the coma is lightening, but as yet there is nothing, those eyes are as dead-looking as the bits of jelly you find washed up on the beach after a storm. Dear Dick, how you would have enjoyed being ministered to by this pert blond creature—just your type—you always had a thing for blondes.

For most of the day Carrie sits by his bedside. She is working a needlepoint tennis racquet cover with her daughter's initials: RAK—Rhee Anne Kurtz. Sometimes she goes through a magazine. Still the conscientious student, she reads *Harper's* and *The Atlantic*. Sometimes she just sits and stares out of the hospital window at the tree-and-house-covered New Jersey hills. I look in on her, but my calendar is jammed today and I don't stay long. We argue pleasantly about who will do supper ("Come on, you're my guests" . . . "Nonsense, let me, for heaven's sake"), and at last she says not to worry, picking up sandwiches at a deli will give her something positive to do. Thus at eight when I come home she is sitting on the terrace next to the pool with a platter of chicken-and-bacon sandwiches and a pitcher of iced tea.

The day is almost gone, the sky, the air is a pale, pale lavender and the pool, too, is a long lavender rectangle, with the tall blue spruce floating in it, and at the tip of the spruce a gold crescent moon and one calm star. I am tired tonight and know that she must be exhausted—this awful waiting is a twilight of its own, a parallel to Dick suspended in sleep—and we don't talk much. There is something about Mina I would like to ask her, but not now, not tonight. I feel about Mina that she is some sort of clue, the key to the puzzle we are living, and that as we proceed through this week, groping through this subterranean dark of crisis, we are somehow groping blindly toward each other. Perhaps this is not correct. I have discovered after three days that talking to Carrie is rather like talking to a wall—oh, a very pleasant, perfectly decorated wall in the simplest, best of taste, but a wall, nevertheless. I sense —perhaps inaccurately—that she is hiding something, a lot of something, and then tell myself I'm looking for clues that probably aren't there. Just because I was unhappy with her husband doesn't mean she has to be. Perhaps they've found in each other a perfect complement: his ambitious restlessness soothed by her cheerful complacency.

Carrie stands up, a big abrupt movement, and takes the plate from my lap and walks toward the kitchen. The light snaps on, turning the air out here black. I watch her through the long glass window, scraping the plates into the sink. The disposal whirrs and grinds, she rinses the plates and dries them. Strange that I feel her action as a usurpation—she is too efficient, too housewifely—this is, after all, my house—but there is something else, a sort of doggedness, a grimness in the way she moves. Maybe she's just tired. I certainly am and I too feel suspended: Jack hasn't called. We have never gone so long a time without speaking to each other. I must go back to the hospital, and on my way through the kitchen (Carrie is putting away the glasses) I see a copy of the Summerville *Sentinel* on the counter. It has obviously been opened and

read. I feel stiff, uneasy. Has she read about the accident and
Kathy?

She has her back to me and her head tilted, looking up at
the cabinet shelf, and suddenly she turns and looks me full in
the face, a pale, defensive, hostile look.

2.

The second time Shaughnessy came out from the city, he took me to see Chekhov's *Uncle Vanya*. All that week, after answering the telephone, after seeing my patients, driving to and from the hospital whenever there was a pause in my schedule, I felt in my gut where usually there is nothing but digestion, a strong, warm, happy ache. Rationally, I knew, of course, that the strange bedding down of the week before had most likely been the happy result of long hunger. Second time round, I was prepared for disappointment. But when the bell rang and I opened my front door and saw him standing there looking palely freckled and apprehensive, with a precise part in his dark red hair, I laughed.

He said, annoyed, "What's so goddam funny?"

Did he think I was laughing at his clothes? In fact, perhaps I was. He was almost too appropriately dressed: white flannel pants, a navy blazer and a pale blue shirt open at the throat. I had expected something less classy in this Irish kid from Queens.

"You're so dressed up," I said.

"Next time," he said, "I'll wear my fig leaf."

We drove to the theater in easy silence. It was one of those gold and green New Jersey evenings when even the endless traffic passes in a blur of sunset colors, and driving there, he kept my hand on his knee, covered with his own. I think we would have done fine, had a jolly evening, but the play was too good, Dr. Astrov played by an excellent actor. "You

know," Astrov said, "when you walk through a forest on a
dark night, if you see a small light gleaming in the distance,
you don't notice your fatigue . . . but for me there is no
small light in the distance." He said this with a terrible sim-
plicity so that I badly wanted to cry. We left the theater without saying anything, and although we had planned to go out
to dinner, Jack drove back to my place instead. I unlocked the
front door, but before I could snap on the hall light Jack's
hand went up to the wall switch and took my hand and I
went into his arms. I could feel his solid damp warmth under
the wool blazer. The side of his neck smelled of after-shave.
We went to the bedroom without turning on the lights; this
time he led me and didn't bump into anything and was so
swift and sure about everything, including the zipper of my
jump suit, that I felt something I hadn't felt for years, ages,
centuries: I felt taken care of, not just my body, which he
cared for very well, but as if he were seeking to know and love
that essence, that speck Quakers call inner light and which
the ancients called a soul.

True Confessions time: One of the things I have always
disliked about myself is a certain overly selective sensuality.
There is a nerve that runs from my medulla oblongata right
to the tip of the clitoris, but in my sad case this nerve is so
choosy that it seldom functions. Let's say that I meet a devas-
tatingly good-looking divorcé at a friend's house one Saturday
night. I come in, he turns. He is tall, dark-haired, dark-eyed,
in a nicely cut sports coat, and he looks a little sad, which
makes it more interesting, and The Nerve—The Nerve is
going boop-boop-a-doop, flashing on and off as vulgarly as a
neon arrow over a bar in Jersey City. We are introduced. I
request from *mein host* two ounces of scotch and four of
soda, we begin to converse. What are your interests, uh, Dan?
He's a tennis player, or worse, a golfer. That's all right with
me, I play tennis, too; we'll give him twenty minutes and see
what else he can come up with. Unfortunately, this hand-

some successful American male hasn't read a book in four years, never goes to the movies, loves musical revivals, thinks the ballet is for pansies, hasn't listened to music since the kids left with their Elton John records, and says proudly that his dog (she got the kids, he got the Labrador) could paint better with his paws than the stuff he sees, not in a gallery, of course, but occasionally reproduced in the Art section of *Time* magazine. Know why she divorced him? He's a bore, that's why, and as soon as I've figured this out (it takes all of twenty-five minutes) that neon nerve begins to blink and fail and I wish I were home with Channel Thirteen. A strange thing happens to the sexes in middle class America. After thirty-five the women get more interesting, the men only make money.

It's not that I'm not sympathetic. I see how the culture made him play with trucks instead of dolls at three and how, at eight, he had to strap on his helmet and cup and fight it out on the ice with the other eight-year-old hockey players, and at sixteen, his parents and girl right there on the bleachers, he put on his shoulder pads and by this time really likes, enjoys, having his brains smushed to grits on the football field. Because, Junior, life is a jungle, and all the things they tell you in Sunday school, Junior, really don't apply. The good old U.S. of A. is a jungle, a heart so dark, so full of mysterious rites to evil gods, weird propitiations, greed, corruption that daily you will either kick or get kicked in the balls and we emphasize football here at Summerville High so that you will learn how to survive. *This* is the wilderness, this pleasant little town of high-priced houses, high-priced gardeners, private schools and country clubs. Junior learns. He sees how, if he's ever going to get a pretty girl and make his pile so that he can afford someday to live in Summerville and repeat the whole generational pattern, he's going to have to take the right courses at the right college and then, of course, get into the "B" school. And then it's a hassle at work, not just earning the daily bread, but getting the right house in the right part of town and, Jesus, the cars, all three of them, and the kids to camp and the club dues. By the time he's forty, he's a real live robot, getting on the 7:20 every day. His ego is inseparable from and interchangeable with his job, and who wants to live with a robot for a lifetime?

Jack isn't like that. He's funny, he's honest, he's normally sensuous, and he not only talks to women he listens to them as well. He doesn't care about having the right house in the right suburb and his tennis game is not country club caliber. But here comes the old ambivalence, why his wife, Nancy, got tired and left. Her college friends all had not just one house, but two, that "big old place" in Rye and the ski house at Stowe or the little old farm in New Hampshire or the place on Martha's Vineyard, and there she was with two kids and a three-room apartment in New York City. And nothing else. And the awful thing is, I understand Nancy. It's hard not to have money. Money is freedom, pleasure, luxury, and here is *my* ambivalence: what worries me about Jack is, does he realize I might someday get tired? I've been working an eighty-hour week for ten years now, and it occurred to me not too long ago that alone, I wouldn't have to do this forever. I've been frugal, I have stocks and savings. I, too, have a little dream. I'd like to buy a piece of a hilltop in Cushing, Maine, where the goldenrod and black-eyed susans grow right down to the sea and you can smell the pungent waters of the bay and the gulls swoop in and out of the horizon, giving their raucous, greedy cries. I would live in a small white house on the top of that hill and work alternately on two books, *Domestic Architecture in America*, and my father's long unfinished work, *A History of Medical Practice*. If I married Jack I might have to hustle forever. And for whom? For his ex-wife and two kids, that's whom. With New Jersey law in its present state of "equality," my dough would of course be his.

Our second date, the night of *Uncle Vanya*, was the night I gave Jack a long comic account of my very first weekend at the Calverson homestead, in the green rolling hills outside of Baltimore. I wonder now at our ability to take pain and transmute it into comic pleasure. But why not? Apes, they say, tell each other jokes, dogs laugh, and all that November weekend, my new husband's mother referred to me as Dr. Kurtz. On Sunday morning, coming down to the living room (it was a lovely house with a wide stairway that curved into a central hall and everywhere inside there was sunlight on silver and mellowed mahogany and everywhere outside there was sunlight snarled in bare treetops), I could hear Jim talking to his mother, who sat in her "peignoir," curled up in a corner of the camelback sofa, smoking. She was a small-boned, pink-faced, white-haired woman with eyes like frozen beebees and a gracious cultured voice that, for me, dripped icicles. Jim was in boots and jodhpurs, having just gone for a little canter at a neighbor's farm. I had looked forward to going, too, but had the uneasy feeling he had gotten up extra early, not waking me so he wouldn't have to display my lack of horsemanship to the hunting crowd.

"Good morning," I said brightly, hoping she would notice the conservative, expensive green tweed dress I'd just-for-her purchased at Abercrombie's.

Clarice looked up. "Why, here's the good doctor," she drawled. The conversation went on, not so much without me as around me—they were talking, as usual, about money. She was asking his advice on investments, and I hope the old bitch took it, Jim being the only bond trader I know who lost money in the market of the sixties. Once or twice during this conversation, Jim's father lumbered through the room, but as if he were invisible, no one batted an eye or turned a head. He was a tall, pale, heavy mussed man who I don't think left the house all weekend. He seemed always to be looking for something, spent a lot of time rooting in drawers and closets, and on the day before, I'd found out why. My unruly body had begun to menstruate, completely unexpectedly, Saturday after lunch. I wasn't sure Clarice had ever menstruated, so instead of asking her for supplies I poked around in the third-floor bedrooms—after all, Jim had had two sisters—and I had finally found my prize, had put my hand into a tall box of Kotex, when instead of the usual texture it struck something sleek and hard, a fifth of bourbon.

The main event that weekend was a Sunday luncheon with some of Jim's old friends and their wives, beginning with bloody Marys at twelve-thirty, on to oyster stew, baked ham and biscuits—all served by a pink-palmed iron-faced black woman whose hostility was so keen that to relieve my racial guilt, I smiled "like a darkie" and humbly said "Thank you" as she served the green beans. She openly sneered, the guests turned their heads and began to jabber. To make up for my *gaffe*, the man at my right lovingly stroked my knee—on only two drinks!—and I had to sit with my right leg crossed over my left under the lace tablecloth just to get away from his fumbly little paw. The men in this crowd were what you'd call good sports, and although I don't remember their faces I do remember their sports coats—a maroon and gray check, a blue and brown plaid, a handsome dark green Harris tweed. The men treated me with a sort of guarded curiosity, but their wives, seeing that I was not the dog they thought a lady doctor should be, fell right into that saccharine-coated female aggressiveness I know so well:

"Why, aren't you just the cleverest thing, a real woman doctor," said Sue Ellen from North Carolina. "I declare, I don't know how you no'then gals do it, you have so much *drahve* and am*b*ition." While in truth, the odor of her ambition, were it not coated with Shalimar, would have knocked you down it was so strong. Not even thirty and that was a real mink jacket she came to lunch in, one of those little fun furs for warm fall days, cut just to be cute, like a sailor's pea coat. Not even thirty and they had a house with stables ("'Course we've only got one little ol' broken-down nag," said Swillin, wrinkling her little nose) and three children, a full-time maid, an *au pair* and out in the Calversons' long gravel driveway, a little ol' fun car, "Poor Bobby's got this borin' hobby, he collects old Rolls," which at first I took to mean something small like cigarette wrappers (she was, after all, from tobacco land) but turned out instead to be a 1926 Silver Shadow. Listen to the other ladies, in true American remnant-puritan style, apologizing like crazy for their dough: "Oh, I know it's silly of us to indulge Kipsy this way," said pretty dark-haired hard-eyed Tipsy, "but finally, I said, 'Go out and get it, sweetie, if it makes you happy,'" (a little Cessna 172) "and I mean, goodness, sometimes it is a nuisance when it's blowing up a storm and you don't know where he's going to crash next; on the other hand," (said solemnly, hand practically over heart) "I think it helps keep the family together. We can pop down to Palm Beach now for a weekend, you see, and isn't it nice for the children to see their grandparents?"

The guests left at three, the drinking went right on. Mr. C (his jacket and tie now off, a dribble of tomato juice decorating his corduroy fly) looked paler and more blotto by the minute, and Clarice was getting meaner, more pink in the face, her eyes turning jelly-bean hard while her head seemed, balloonlike, to swell. It was hot for November and humid, and bingo, exactly at six, inside and out, we had a thunderstorm.

"I can' believe this!" yelled Clarice from the kitchen, where her gracious voice was beginning to scotch final consonants. "Wher' all the damn bread go? Jus' bought a loaf yesterday."

I felt a terrible pang of guilt. *J'accuse!* Had I eaten it in my sleep? Finished off her Pepperidge Farm?

Came Mr. C's rumble-mumble from the den.

"Well, I'll tell you wha' all the shouting about," cried Clarice. "I haven't paid the Market in two months, and by God, I'm thurly sick of goin' in there with my chin up, pretending I don' know how much I owe, and here we are out of bread and I haven't paid the phone bill and Sally, that bish, says she's leaving this week unless I scrape up some cash.

Will, Will! Do you hear me? CASH." The fight went on, both contestants scoring points. *He* had paid that big bill at Hutzler's, who in hell did she think she was, Jackie K? And she, out of her teensy-weensy inheritance had paid the mortgage. God, if she'd ever thought when she'd met him that they'd be living on *her* dough. Their voices rose and fell—incredible pitches and dips of hatred and loathing. Just after an especially loud thunderclap, I thought the house had been hit, but no, turned out that she had thrown a glass; next the sound of a loud thud, the size, say, of Volume 14 of the Britannica, followed by a crash (lamplike) and a shriek, "You son-of-a-bish, my mother's Waterford," and a yowl thereupon like a werewolf at midnight. He bellowed, she screamed—by God, a good old upper middle class American ruckus. I slipped out of the house—if I gave medical aid, would they later sue?—and stood on the gravel drive, coatless in the driving rain. Presently, Jim joined me in a trench coat, his face composed into a square-jawed mask. I should have felt something for him, I could see him, a square-jawed little nine-year-old stuffing his head under the pillow while mums and daddy brawled, but he said now, without sadness, or irony, or feeling of any kind, except maybe put-outedness (the trace of a pout along his lips), "Well, pet, there goes din-din. Shall we eat at the Club?"

I whined, my stomach lurching, "Can't we just grab a sandwich at a diner?"

He said that he, at least, was very hungry and at the Club he could sign a chit. Or, he said, ironically, did I happen to have a few dollars on me, as the whole blooming weekend, my new dress included, had cost a bundle, dear, and he was broke.

The rain fell on my head, on my neck, on my itchy tweed shoulders. It streamed down my cheeks with the force of a revelation, a regular Baptist dip-in. I had a sudden awful premonition. Stuck with his upper middle class life, would I, in ten or twenty years, be somewhere in horse country boozing it up and screeching? I had married him, I thought, for some kind of family life. James Calverson, scion of twelve generations of Calversons (with just a little glossed-over Jewish money on his mother's mother's side) and all that rooted, generational background. Was I, instead of some real roots and a little belongingness, getting a stage set from a *New Yorker* magazine liquor ad? Right there, two months married, I should have quit, but I am a poor quitter and instead stuck it out for two more stage-set years. And right there in the driving rain, my new expensive wool tweed dress stuck to my clavicles, I had the funniest feeling: that Jim Calverson had married Dr. Kurtz so that he'd be well taken care of.

Jack laughed. It was 1 A.M. that evening of *Uncle Vanya* and we were cooking dinner. In lieu of an apron he had a tea towel stuck into his belt and was briskly sprinkling garlic salt on the salad. Then he put down the shaker and frowned.

"So?" he said.

"So?" I said. "What do you mean, so? So what?"

"Why does that bother you so much?" He looked up. There was something pugnacious in the way he'd said this—a very slight thrust of his square jaw.

I can play games, too, and I coyly returned, "Why does what bother me?"

"Why did it bother you that he wanted to be taken care of?"

"I meant, financially."

"Okay. Financially."

I stared at Jack and then shrugged. "Nobody likes to think they're being used."

"How was Calverson using you? Maybe *you* were using *him*. You were living in his apartment, right?"

"Right."

"In a place you couldn't have afforded on your resident's salary, right?"

"Right, but that's not why I married him."

"You sure? You know what I see looking around this house?"

"What?"

"Lots of very good taste. Good taste is expensive. I know, since I was once married to someone with very good taste."

"Is that why you broke up? You couldn't afford her?"

"Hey, she can be very nasty."

"You asked for it. What I do with the money I earn is my business."

"All right. I'm just curious. If he was such a jerk, why did you marry him?"

"I was lonely."

"And there was no one else around? In the whole city of New York?"

"Well—"

"Go on. Tell me about it. I'm very interested."

"He seemed so—"

"What? Rich?"

"Not rich, exactly. Settled. Well set up. In a way, glamorous. He did have good taste, a lovely apartment, interesting New York friends. All right, there is that side of me. I can appreciate style too, you know."

"Oh, I know." There was something mocking in his voice and a wary gleam in his brown-gold eyes.

"Wait a minute," I said. "You're not being fair. Your ex-wife doesn't exactly sound like a character out of "The Lower Depths.""

"Not at all," he said.

"Then what are you getting all hot about?" I shoved the steak under the broiler. "You know what your trouble is?"

"Tell me, Doctor. What?"

"You're ambivalent as hell."

"About what?"

"About what you want out of life. You want to think of yourself as Shaughnessy the writer—hey, folks, look at me! I'm not middle class like the rest of you poor fools, and yet, oh boy, do you admire some of those middle class things you sneer at."

"Maybe, but not enough to marry for them."

"No? Then tell me just what it was that attracted you to Nancy?"

"She was, for one thing, exceptionally pretty."

Something, an icicle of pain, slipped through my left lung. Often lately I didn't feel pretty. "Is she a blonde?"

"Nancy? No. She's got black hair and blue eyes."

"She's Irish?"

"And German."

I looked up. "And rich?"

He was grudging. "Her family's well off."

"That figures. I mean, if you're divorced and she lives in Larchmont."

"I don't get the point of this," he said. He jerked the tea towel out of his belt and laid it on the counter.

"The point is, maybe one of the things you liked about her is what you like about me."

"That you're pretty?" he said, but coldly, so that it felt like he meant the opposite.

"Maybe I'm not pretty but at least I'm not—a dependent. I have some means. You know? Like, money."

He leaned across the counter, almost menacingly. "You're saying I like your money the way I liked Nancy's money?"

"Isn't that what you just said to me? About Jim Calverson?" We stood facing each other, squared off. And then his shoulders relaxed.

"This is dumb, Nell. What are we fighting for?"

"I don't know. You started it."

"You started it," he said in a high teeny five-year-old voice.

"Dammit," I said, trying not to smile. "You're the most . . . Hand me that potholder, will you?" A cloud of black smoke had come curling out of the oven. I pulled out the broiler pan, flopped over the black-crusted, sizzling steak.

"It's hopeless, anyway," Jack said gloomily, "analyzing the past. Why you did what when."

"I'm not sure about that. I keep hoping that analytical intelligence will save us all from making the same mistakes over and over."

"I doubt it," he said. He sat down at the kitchen table and wearily rubbed his eyes with his fists, like a little kid. "I don't really believe that. I believe in doing what you think you want to do."

"Despite mistakes?"

"I'd rather risk a thousand mistakes than sit around analyzing forever. Everybody makes mistakes. There's no such thing as a perfect life."

"And you a Catholic."

"Not a good one."

"I wouldn't like you if you were."

"I know it."

"How do you know that?"

"You don't trust religious feeling."

"You're right. Was Nancy a Catholic?"

"A poor one. Like me. That smell you smell is the steak burning. Dammit. You're right, Nell, I'm just the same as you. The first time I saw Nancy she had on a blue cashmere sweater that matched her eyes and little gold earrings. I was so proud of her. Me, Jack Shaughnessy, had this classy girl. And her house—Jesus, a pool, and a kitchen you could roast an ox in, and the bedrooms, five kids and they all had rooms of their own. Why was it she made me feel like such a failure? I thought I was earning a lot of money, but where did it all go? I couldn't understand it. I was earning four times what my father earned and it was never enough. Shouldn't you feel like a success if you're earning more than your father? And here were Arthur and Bobby on their policemen's salaries contributing to the folks and I never had a penny. I wasn't even doing what I wanted to do, just plugging along, trying to pay the bills."

I put the steak on the cutting board and sliced it—flash-cut, flash-cut. Upward and Onward. The story of Western Civilization. Père Goriot.

"What the hell did she expect? She didn't marry a rich man, she knew that. It got so bad—ach, I don't know. After work, I just couldn't face going home. I used to stop in at a little bar on Third Avenue, and one day there was a girl there —not a girl, a woman from the office, a nice comfortable woman she was, divorced, no airs; she seemed to like me when it had gotten so bad I didn't even like myself."

I fixed our plates and brought them to the table. I put down forks and knives and paper napkins. I poured out two glasses of red wine. Jack was sitting still, looking down at the table.

"Hey," I said. He lifted his eyes. They were red-rimmed. "You're right. Let's not analyze. Eat your nice dinner, Jack. You know what let's do tomorrow if it's sunny?"

He smiled, a weakly lecherous smile.

"That too," I said rapidly, "but first we'll go for a drive. Take a picnic somewhere, all right? There's a little park I know down in Pennsylvania, in upper Bucks County. It's very pretty, not like a city park—meadows and woods, that kind of stuff. I like you, Jack. Do you like me?"

"Yeah. I'm afraid so."

"Jack."

"What?"

"I have something to ask you."

"What?"

"Do you think I'm pretty?"

3.

It is late, very late, yet I dawdle at the hospital, spend extra amounts of time with each patient, chat with the nurses, stop for a cup of coffee at the snack bar and finally, sometime after eleven, head for home, hoping Carrie will be fast asleep or pretending to be. But even before I open the door I hear the snuffle and roar of my asthmatic Hoover. Carrie is vacuuming.

"Hello!" I shout. She turns, looking scared, and jerks the plug.

"Gracious," she says, "you startled me. I hope you don't mind my doing this. I just felt like doing something. How is Dick?"

"Still the same. I'm going to have some tea, would you like some?"

She follows me out to the kitchen and stands there in her bare feet and wrap skirt, staring into space. The fluorescent light makes her pale face look slightly green. I put the kettle on and there is the Summerville *Sentinel* right where I'd left it. I wish it would go away. I wish she would go away. I am tired and have troubles of my own.

She says, "I used the phone. I called the children."

"That's fine," I say.

"Rhee lost her tennis match. Jeff fell at the pool and cut his lip."

"Lips heal easily," I tell her.

"Did you know her? That Harrington girl?"

I am doing things very mechanically now, setting out two cups on saucers, getting the tea bags.

"I did know her. She was a patient of mine. I wrote a letter for her when she applied to nursing school."

"How awful," she murmurs. "She was only a few years older than Phil." She sits down on a high kitchen stool and hooks her knitted fingers around her knees. What does her posture remind me of? Something from Goya? A dunce-capped fool? A little girl who is always good? "The way the story was written, made it look as if . . ." She bites her lip. Steam rises from the kettle. Carefully, using a potholder, I pour the water into the cups. I do not raise my eyes.

"I don't understand how it happened. Another car jumped the barrier, went the wrong way down the highway, Dick swerved to avoid him, crashed, and the other car—completely disappeared? It's incredible. Three other motorists saw the car but not one of them could tell the model or color?"

"That highway is very dark."

"Do you think I should call her family?"

Is she kidding? No, she's not.

"No," she says, "I'll write a note. He must have been giving her a ride home. You see, he's been working on a special project and Saturday night one of his patients went into a coma, so they called him at home. The Harrington girl must have been sick or without transportation."

I can't think of anything to say, at least nothing that is both honest and kind.

She says, "You look so strange, Nell."

"Do I? I'm just tired."

"You don't think much of Dick, do you?"

"Carrie, you have to remember that my marriage to Dick ended badly."

"We've discussed it, you know."

"What?"

"Your marriage. I mean, your marriage to Dick."

"I'm sure you have," I say, and have a sudden image of

them lying in bed together, after a little sex, discussing, "our marriage." Dick would be good at that. Did he tell her that I was frigid? Sloppy? Coldhearted? What?

"I understand why you'd be suspicious. Dick told me about that nurse."

"What nurse?" I ask, honestly curious.

"You know. The one he fell in love with, just after you were married."

"Oh." I can't help smiling. So that's his version. I might have known it would be something like that. He simply fell out of love with me. When, in fact, I doubt whether he's ever loved anyone. Dick is the sort of man to whom marriage is the ultimate convenience—convenient sex, convenient domestic arrangements—a presentable wife, kids, house. What really matters to him is his career. No, I don't think he loved that nurse. He might have slept with her, but I doubt he loved her.

Carrie gets up. "Thanks for the tea," she says. "I guess I'll go to bed. I've got to go home for a while tomorrow, just to check on things. Oh. I forgot to tell you. Jack Shaughnessy called. Good night."

For the next two hours I try to get Jack on the telephone, but there is no answer. Early in the morning, at six or so, I try again. Out. Obviously out all night. Up in Larchmont with Nancy? Do they, I wonder, occasionally sleep together? I lie in bed looking up at the white ceiling speckled with light and shade. Another day to get through. My eyes feel gritty, my bones ache. I feel old and empty and tired. Why get up? I think. What's the point? Dozens of people to see and all of them needing sympathy, attention, help, care and I am so tired and there is no one in the world who cares that I am tired. I would like to sleep and sleep . . . I wake up again at eight, already late to see patients. Carrie has left for Ellerton. At the hospital, I hear from the starched blond nurse that just twenty minutes ago Dr. Kurtz woke up. Opening his eyes, he looked up at her and said, "Paula?"

FOUR

1.

"His name is Kurtz," Mina said. "Dick Kurtz. He's Buzz's roommate. Buzz says he's a fantastic guy. Not that I trust Buzz's judgment."

They were on the Van Duynes' back porch and it was June, two days before Mina's fourteenth birthday. School had been out a week, Clay had been home from Andover for two weeks, Buzz had been home from Princeton for three weeks and would leave Monday for Maine, where he had a job as a sailing instructor at a camp. Upstairs they could hear Clay's radio playing something twangy and Western. In the garden the asparagus was up, the tomatoes planted, rows of ruby and green lettuce alternated like strung beads and Mrs. Van Duyne in a faded blue dress and large straw hat was weeding: stooping, rising, stooping again. Already the June air breathed summer's warmth, bees' droning, the smell of earth, expectation and listlessness.

"Or," Mina said, "there's Clay's roommate. His name is John Collier and he's from West Virginia. Clay swears he's the greatest guy who ever lived." Mina sat up, folding her long, already tanned legs under her and putting a hand on each knee, gently swayed back and forth so that the old porch glider groaned rustily—oh! ah! Nell sat on the porch floor with her legs out straight and her back against a post.

"I'd ask you to stay over Saturday night," Mina said, "but Julia's coming home with the twins. They're going to have my old room, she's going to move in with me. We're all going to have dinner here, though, before the dance. You, too, of course."

Nell straightened her back and sighed.

"Well?" Mina said.

"I don't know," Nell said carefully. "It sounds like fun, and since it's your birthday . . ."

"Oh, I know," Mina said. "I'll bet you're going to Carrie's for the weekend."

"No," Nell said. "Though she did ask me for Sunday night. She's gone to New Hampshire to visit her grandmother."

"Well, damn," Mina said, swinging her legs out in front of her. She had on dirty white tennis shorts and a white T-shirt three sizes too large. Mina was tall, thin, round-shouldered, flat-chested, beautiful. "I ought to give up on you, Nell. What do you see in that dull, dull girl?"

"Carrie's not dull."

"Miss Goody Two-shoes," Mina said scornfully. "I can't bear that little act of hers. She thinks she's Mrs. Miniver."

Nell laughed. "Okay," she said, "what does that make you?" Mina had grown from tomboyhood into perpetual moody rebellion. She would date anyone in town just for laughs, the creepiest characters, Tony Gardella for instance— short, bandy-legged Tony whose slick black hair and dirty fingernails made Nell cringe and whose flat-nosed face was a seething mass of acne pustules. Mina took a firm hand with Tony, told him he was a lot of laughs, called him Tony-o, rode all the way to Albany on the back of his motorcycle. She went out with Jake Jakowski and the Mill Street crowd, who would take a case of beer and a pile of blankets out to the quarry on a Saturday night. The Van Duynes had discussed sending Mina to boarding school. "Terrific," Mina said, "it's into the nunnery. Mina's been a bad widdle durl so she gets to go where it's lights-out at ten and there's lots of healthful oatmeal for breakfast. Let's save my virginity, everybody." "I just don't know what to do with Mina," Mrs. Van Duyne would say, smiling and shaking her head.

"Who's Clay taking?"

"Clay who? Oh, you mean my brother Clay? I get it, you want to go with *him*. No kidding, I never figured that."

"I guess if he wanted to ask me, he would."

"Not necessarily. Clay's kind of slow."

"I'll bet he likes Carrie."

"No, he doesn't, he thinks she's a horse."

"How do you know? He'd never say that to you."

"I just know. I think he's scared of you because you're pretty."

"Blah."

"No, seriously, if Clay asks you, will you go?"

"Maybe, if he asks me."

"Terrific," Mina said. "Buzz is taking Cissy Taylor. I heard him describe her to Clay as having a pneumatic thorax. Isn't he nice? You don't have a cigarette, do you? I'm dying for a butt."

"No," Nell said.

"It's really nice that your parents are having a trip to New York," Mina said.

"Yeah," Nell said.

"How's your father doing? Is he feeling better?"

"Not really," Nell said.

"New York will do him good," Mina said. She suddenly stood up (the glider plaintively groaned) and stretched. "Oh God, someday I'm going to get out of this stupid two-bit town. Can you imagine living here forever? Marrying some local jerk and having kids, going to meetings at church and parties at the Masonic Hall and the annual Sportsman's Dinner and getting drunk at the Club on Saturday nights? Je-*sus*, I want to get out of here so *badly*. I want to go to London and Paris and Rome and see everything there is to see. You know something, Nell, I'm never going to get married. I'm going to live all alone and travel and write terrific books." She laughed, made a fist and banged the clapboard side of the porch. "Hey. Let's go downtown and see who's at Schuller's.

Jimmy Atkins' cousin is in town. I saw him the other day, playing tennis. He's fantastic-looking, six-one with dark hair and the most divine blue eyes. The only thing is, he wears braces." Mina looked at Nell and made a noisy smacking sound with her lips and Nell laughed. They had written a radio script together for eighth grade English class about two kids dating who wanted to kiss but didn't know how to remove their glasses or braces. Miss Ensin, their buck-toothed English teacher, had tried to smile but had blushed angrily instead. Afterward, Miss Ensin had said to the class, "Another Mina Van Duyne production," although the script had been Nell's idea. Mina's reputation always preceded her.

Nell, with Carrie's tennis racquet balanced across the handlebars, rode her bike to the back of the Pettigrew house and parked it on the terrace. Mrs. Pettigrew was lying on the wrought-iron chaise, in a two-piece pink bathing suit, reading a novel. From ten yards you would have thought she was sixteen, her figure was still so good, and the sun picked out all the red in her dark hair. She looked up at Nell over her sunglasses. "Hi, Nell," she said. "Isn't this a lovely day? Carrie's in the kitchen."

Carrie was rinsing out a mixing bowl as Nell came through the door.

"Hey," Nell said, "it's too hot to be in here cooking."

"Hey, Nell," Carrie said, "you didn't have to bring that right back. I can always use my mom's racquet."

"That's okay," Nell said, and laid the racquet on the countertop. "What're you doing?"

"Baking a chocolate chip cake. It's my father's favorite. What's new with you?"·

"Nothing much. I lost."

"Gee, that's too bad. Who did you play?"

"Alison Snyder."

"She likes to lob."

"I know it. I hate her kind of game."

"So do I but she keeps on winning. You seem sort of quiet and depressed today."

"Do I? I'm not really."

"You going to the dance at the Club?"

"I don't know. Nobody's asked me and it's getting late."

"I thought Clay might ask you."

"Clay? Why?"

"He's always watching you. You know? Like this." Carrie squinted her blue eyes and made them go slyly sideways so that Nell smiled. She liked Carrie a lot and didn't understand why Carrie and Mina couldn't get along anymore. Probably because of that Billy business. He had liked Carrie first, but Mina, on purpose it seemed, had flirted with him and gotten him to take her out.

Carrie hiked herself up on the countertop and Nell did too, and the girls sat across from each other, swinging their legs and smiling. Carrie had on shorts, too, but wore a man's white shirt with the sleeves torn out. Just this last year she had grown large round breasts and she wouldn't wear T-shirts. She was broad-shouldered and full-bosomed, with slim hips and firm slim legs. She wasn't pretty, but had an appealing smile and had been voted "Nicest" girl in the eighth grade.

"How's your father doing?" Carrie asked.

"About the same," Nell said, looking down at the new red brick vinyl floor. Just this last year, Mrs. Pettigrew had had her kitchen done over again. The kitchen door swung open and Mrs. Pettigrew in a pink sundress with white rickrack trim stood looking in at them. "I'm off, tootsie," she said. "Think you can handle things?"

"Oh, sure," Carrie said. "Say 'Hi' to Aunt Ethel for me. Drive carefully, okay?"

"Always," Mrs. Pettigrew said, and blew Carrie a kiss. "I'll be back before six."

"Have a good time," Carrie called out as the door swung shut. In a minute they heard her car go out of the drive.

"What about you?" Nell asked. "Aren't you going to the dance?"

Carrie blinked her pale lashes and smiled. "Well, so far nobody's asked me, either."

"Even if somebody did ask me," Nell said, "I doubt I'd go. I'd have to get a new dress."

The buzzer on the stove went off and Carrie slid off the counter. Just as she bent to look in the oven, Mr. Pettigrew, looking very hot and flushed, came in through the side door. "Where's your mother?" he asked, not even saying hello.

Carrie's blue eyes looked startled. "She just left, Daddy. She's gone up to Saratoga to have lunch with Aunt Ethel."

"Goddammit," Mr. Pettigrew said. He stood in the middle of the kitchen with his hands on his hips and his head down, looking like a basketball player who has just missed his free shot.

"What's wrong, Daddy?" Carrie asked anxiously.

"What?" Mr. Pettigrew said, raising his head. "Oh, nothing, nothing baby, don't you worry. What time is she coming back, did she say?"

"Before six," Carrie said. Her lips looked pale.

Mr. Pettigrew smiled in a funny way.

"I'm cooking dinner tonight," Carrie said. "We're having all your favorite things."

"That's terrific, sweetie," Mr. Pettigrew said. His eyes looked sweaty in his red face and he turned and went back out the door, and then his car zoomed out of the drive.

Nell slid off the counter. "Guess I'd better go," she said. "Want to go downtown for a while?"

"I can't," Carrie said. "I've got to finish this. Thanks, anyway."

"Yeah," Nell said. "Well, I'll see you."

"Okay," Carrie said. She opened the oven door. "Perfecto," she said. A gust of hot, chocolate-scented air filled the kitchen and Nell, who was thin, but always dieting and always hungry, felt nauseous.

"Sure you won't come?" she asked again.

"Oh no, no, thanks," Carrie said. Nell went back out through the dining room and the living room to the terrace. She stood for a while looking at the Pettigrews' beautiful garden with its little formal beds of flowers and roses. She didn't know what to do. She didn't want to go downtown and she didn't want to go home. Maybe she'd go downtown and just look at dresses in Jordan's and maybe just try one on.

Late that afternoon when Nell came in, Mrs. Dreher was sitting at the kitchen table. She had her letter-writing things spread out on the yellow oilcloth: thin airmail stationery, an old shoebox in which she kept letters and the backs of envelopes with addresses on them. Every week she wrote a dozen letters—to her sisters in East Germany, to her aunts in Heidelberg, to cousins in Berlin and Cologne. She always gave Nell the news she received in her letters—who had gotten married and who had died and who had had babies. But these relationships, which Mrs. Dreher had kept alive over so many turbulent years, meant nothing to Nell. These cousins and aunts and second cousins were less real to her than the people she read about in newspapers or books.

Nell sat down across from her mother at the table and began plucking off one by one green grapes from a bunch in a wooden bowl. When she pulled off a grape, fruit flies rose from the bowl in a panic and then settled down again. Her mother looked up at Nell, pen poised in hand, then her lips moved, her eyes became glassy, she bent her head and wrote.

"Oh," said Mrs. Dreher, glancing up, "before I forget. Clay Van Duyne called. He said he would call again this evening."

Nell frowned and shrugged one shoulder. "I guess it's about the Club dance Saturday night."

"Ah," Mrs. Dreher said, smiling. She sighed, put down the pen, folded the thin tissue paper in thirds and slipped it into the airmail envelope.

"I don't know if I'll go or not. He's a little late."

"He is perhaps shy," said Mrs. Dreher. "If you go, you must have a new dress."

Nell shrugged again and sat with her chin in her hands, looking down at a cigarette burn on the oilcloth.

"A pretty eyelet dress, perhaps. I saw a nice dress in Jordan's, not too expensive. *Ach, ya,* it's nice to be young. Nell. Don't say anything about your father, all right?"

"Everybody knows he's sick, Mother."

"But not how he's sick. We'll see what Dr. Edelstein says. I trust him. He was a leading doctor in Berlin. *Ach, Gott,* we can't go on this way. Some days I think your father's mind has completely gone. I don't know. How are we going to live? On what?" She addressed this question not to Nell but to the kitchen window, where a soft light, the gauzy pink of a dance dress, rubbed against the screen. Nell sat still, her chin in her hands.

"Nevertheless," Mrs. Dreher said cheerfully, "there are still a few pennies left. Do Mina and Carrie go too?"

"Mina's going," Nell said. "Listen, I really don't even want to go."

"Of course you should go. Now when you're young you should have a good time." And she smiled at Nell tenderly and Nell frowned and looked away. She understood how her mother was always caught between the truth and illusion of their lives, that there was no money now that Dr. Dreher was sick and yet how much she wanted Nell to have a good time, and Nell, on her side, in reciprocity, so often pretended not to know how bad things were, pretended to have a good time so that her mother would at least not need to worry about her.

Mrs. Dreher took off her reading glasses and rubbed the bridge of her nose with a thumb and forefinger. "Who would have thought it, eh?" she asked of no one in particular.

In the hall, Dr. Dreher was standing at the mirror that hung over a little table, looking at himself. As Nell passed he said, "How do I look to you?"

In fact, he looked old, ancient, seventy at least. He had lost weight and shrunk, his face sagged, there was something missing in his blue eyes: they looked dead.

"Fine," Nell said. "You look fine."

"Fine," Dr. Dreher said to himself in the mirror. "Fine, fine, fine."

Nell went upstairs to her room and shut the door.

For twenty years, Dr. Johann Dreher, a general practitioner, had in his spare time been writing a history of medical practice from Dioscorides to the present. But just last year, he had suddenly lost interest in his almost completed work. Notebooks, clippings, papers, were stacked in dusty piles on top of his filing cases. If Nell went into his study now to announce "Dinner" she would find him sitting in his chair, staring at the walls, or sitting at his desk with his head in his hands, or lying on his leather sofa, staring up at the ceiling.

He was a man of medium size with a rosy, rather cherubic face, a pink polished bald head with a monklike fringe of white hair. He had always been eccentric, but lately he had become difficult. He couldn't sleep at night, and at three or four in the morning, Nell would hear him just coming up the stairs or perhaps getting up and going down. He became absent-minded, couldn't remember little everyday facts. If you said to him, "My, it's a nice day," he would stare at you and say, "Of course you know that in 1933 . . ."

One day as Nell sat across from him at breakfast, he called her Lotte, his sister's name. On a sunny day in May, he put on his winter overcoat, hat, earmuffs and plaid scarf. Dressed for a snowstorm, he drove to the hospital. He couldn't remember people's names—the names of those he knew in the present began to be replaced by the names of those he had known, who were dead. Once when Nell went into his study to use his big dictionary, she found inserted in the old black German typewriter a sheet of paper which said:

Dreher, Gerhardt		Schumann, Luise	
b. 1860	d. 1914	b. 1868	d. 1921
b. 1890 Josef		d. 1916 Russian front	
b. 1892 Ella		d. 1918 Influ.	
b. 1893 Maria		d. 1921 TB	
b. 1895 Walther		d. 1945 Dresden	
b. 1897 Karl		d. 1943 Tobruk	
b. 1899 Lotte		d. 1944? Belsen	
b. 1901 Johann		d. ?	
b. 1903 Lise		d. 1945 Shot by Russians	

Four years after World War II, a letter had come from the International Red Cross saying that after long and diligent effort they had been able to establish that Charlotte Dreher Spurmann, her husband and two sons had died at the Belsen Concentration Camp sometime after 1944 and that Lise Marthe Dreher von Kurwitz-Hagdorf and her husband, Count Theodor Ernst von Kurwitz-Hagdorf, had been shot by invading Russian troops on their estate near Kuhlsdorf, Mecklenburg. Nell's father went into his study and shut the door. Mrs. Dreher, who never cried, stood at the window, looking out at the twilit street as Nell came in. It was a kind, middle-American street of maple trees, spattered pink and green light, and soft early evening voices. Up the street someone was mowing a lawn, and across the street, old Mrs. Ferguson was calling her dog for supper. "Morgan, Morgan," she called. Mrs. Dreher turned and, looking at Nell with dry tired eyes, said, "I can no longer believe in God."

Afterward, Dr. Dreher seemed changed. He was less alert, more hesitant. His mind seemed to stumble, picking its way like a wounded man hobbling across a lot full of bombed-out rubble. His senses began to fail—he seemed not to see well, didn't hear. Time lost its organization; history—his own, the world's—was chaos. His mind had begun to wander.

"Good morning, good morning, good morning!" Dr. Dreher shouted at Nell when she came down for breakfast on Saturday morning. He sat at the table in a gray summer suit, vest, white shirt, tie and raincoat. "Wonderful morning! *Schönes Wetter! Heute machen wir eine Reise!*"

"Speak English, Hans," Mrs. Dreher said. She put a glass of orange juice down on the table for Nell and a cup of tea in front of Dr. Dreher. Mrs. Dreher had on a yellow linen suit and very red lipstick.

"*Was ist das?*" Dr. Dreher inquired, looking at the tea as if it were a curiosity.

"Tea," Mrs. Dreher said, poured herself a cup of coffee and sat down. She said to Nell, "You're going to play tennis today?"

Dr. Dreher said, "*Tee? Aber warum? Wo ist mein Kaffee?*"

Mrs. Dreher sighed, looked at Nell and said, "For twenty years he's had tea for breakfast every morning. Now, today, he wants coffee." She got up, removed the cup with a jerk so that tea slopped into the saucer.

"*Vielen, vielen Dank,*" Dr. Dreher said, rubbing his hands as the steaming coffee was put before him. "*Man muss jeden Morgen guten Kaffee trinken.*"

Nell drank her orange juice and looked out of the window. It was a perfect June day, perfect for tennis, perfect for dancing. Last night, she dreamed that she had married Clay Van Duyne and they had gone to live in the Van Duyne house. When they came through the front door, she saw that the house was completely empty. There was no furniture in it, or rugs or draperies, and the air was cold and dusty. Clay had locked the door behind him and turned to her, smiling. He was dressed in winter clothes—ski clothes. Looking down, she saw that she had nothing on. "Oh! Excuse me," she said, and ran into another room. She began to run from room to room and he chased her, smiling all the while, his ski boots clomping through the empty house. She was afraid that he would catch her and afraid that he wouldn't.

"Did you have pleasant dreams?" Mrs. Dreher asked, smiling at her.

"—Uh," Nell said, "I never dream." She broke off a bit of toast and fed it to Taffy, who sat at attention next to her chair. The dog sniffed the toast—what? no jam?—took it delicately between her lips and dropped it on the floor.

"*Welchen Weg nehmen wir?*" Dr. Dreher asked Mrs. Dreher. "*Wie schön ist es im Frühling eine Reise zu machen! Natürlich gehen wir nach Bayern!*"

"Hans, I told you," Mrs. Dreher said. "We are going to New York City to see Dr. Edelstein. Remember? He is going to examine you. You are going to the hospital for some tests."

"Edelstein?" His face cleared, he beamed and he said in German, "My old friend Edelstein. What's wrong with him?" Then he turned to Nell and said, still in German, "And what are you going to do today, Lotte?"

Mrs. Dreher sighed.

Nell stood up. "When are you leaving?"

"Soon," Mrs. Dreher said. "We're all ready. Oh, Nell. Another thing. Lock the doors. That Gorshak woman comes all the time now and just stands and looks at the house. I don't know what she wants. Poor thing, ever since the boy was killed, she wanders all over town."

"Maybe it's his ghost making her do it," Nell said. "Maybe she pushed him into that swimming pool."

"Pushed her own son into an empty pool? No, no. Maybe he fell, maybe some boys did it. You must understand: the boy was all she had. Now be a good girl, Nell, and have a nice time at the dance tonight."

"Sure," Nell said. "Don't speed on the highway."

"What?" Mrs. Dreher said jokingly. "Can't I have any fun?"

"*Siehst du,*" Dr. Dreher said to Mrs. Dreher in German, "my sister is going to marry a count." He leaned confidentially toward Mrs. Dreher and said, "I'll tell you something, he's not only rich and well educated, he's an awfully nice fellow. My beautiful little sister! If only my parents could have lived, if only, if only," and suddenly, like a record running down, he stopped.

Mrs. Dreher stood up. "We're back from 1927," she said dryly. Dr. Dreher looked at his coffee cup and said in English to Mrs. Dreher, "You have made a mistake again. You gave me coffee. You know I never drink coffee."

As they pulled out of the driveway, Mrs. Dreher in hat and white gloves was looking fearlessly ahead over the steering wheel and Dr. Dreher, next to her on the front seat, sat waving at Nell out of the car window. His round cheeks were shiny with tears.

Mrs. Van Duyne was on the telephone as Nell came through the kitchen door.

"No, he isn't, Mary," she was saying. "He's over at the Club playing tennis. It's not urgent, is it? . . . Oh, I see. . . . Yes, I'll tell him. . . . Umm-hmm. . . . Um-hmm. . . . Yes, I will. Tell me before you hang up how your mother's feeling. . . . She is? Well, that's just grand. I'm delighted to hear it. Give her my love, will you? Good-bye, dear. Tell me something, Nell," she said, hanging up the receiver. "Does my hair look funny?"

"Gee, no," Nell said. "It looks great. I've never seen it like that before."

Mrs. Van Duyne sighed, opened the corner cupboard and took out a cracked hand mirror. She held the mirror first this way and then that, studying herself critically. "This is all your mother's fault," she said sternly to Nell. "I saw her at a church meeting this week and she said to me very severely, 'Henrietta, you must go to the hairdresser.' So here I am, with my hair up like Madame Pompadour. I feel as if I dasn't move my head. Oh, your mother will have me all straightened out before long. She says she's going to take me shopping for new clothes and that I'm to hire a cleaning lady. Can you imagine? Dr. Van Duyne would have a stroke. Did they get off to New York City?"

"Just now," Nell said.

"And how's your father feeling?"

"Well, not so good, I guess."

Mrs. Van Duyne turned her lovely light sympathetic eyes on Nell. "I'm so sorry, Nell." Then her eyes swept away and she said, "You know, I'm getting rattled. Let's see, there'll be ten of us tonight for dinner—Buzz's friend Dick isn't coming. Ten's not so bad, only three more than usual. I thought I'd have lemon chicken with parsley sauce and a strawberry short-cake for a birthday cake."

"You don't know where Mina is, do you? We're supposed to play tennis."

"Are you?" Mrs. Van Duyne said, surprised. "That's funny. She left a little while ago. I saw her go out toward the woods. Maybe she took the shortcut to the Club."

"We were going to play at the public courts."

"Isn't that odd? She never forgets tennis dates. Maybe having a birthday confused her. I'd go out back to look for her. She doesn't seem in a very good mood today. Here I thought being fourteen would cure her moods."

Darn you, Mina, Nell thought, what's the matter with you, anyway? Even if it is your birthday, I don't want to spend it hunting for you. She walked around Mrs. Van Duyne's garden, past the barn and into the sudden pine-scented coolness of the woods. And I know what you're doing, too, she thought. You're out there grabbing a butt. We're lucky you haven't burned the woods down.

Once, when Nell had been particularly angry at Mina for one of her moods, she had flared up at her and said, "Who do you think you are, acting like that? What gives you the right to act like that?" And Mina, equally angry, had said, "I'll act any damn way I please." Which was exactly what annoyed Nell the most—that arrogance of hers, her attitude which said, I'll do anything I want, and all of it came out of having so much—a family everyone thought was marvelous, a lovely home, beauty, brains too, but most of all the fact that the Van Duynes had lived here for two hundred years ("Two hundred years?" Nell's mother had said. "What's that? A drop in time's bucket.") and thought they owned everything. Like these woods, for instance. The woods weren't even their woods, although the Van Duynes acted as if they were. Last year, a new Democratic mayor had discovered that the woods really belonged to the town and the woods had instantly been sold to Dugan and Giordanno, Contractors. Now, every morning, the Van Duynes woke up to the dull roar of bulldozers half a mile away. Dugan and Giordanno were busy tearing up the hillside, putting up tiny houses in pastel colors like Jordan almonds, each tiny house with a huge silver TV aerial on its roof. Wasn't life funny? Nell's mother said, laughing. Here was old Bud Dugan, the town drunk, reformed by AA and well on his way to making a fortune. Nice for Susie and her brother, said Mrs. Dreher, but someday everyone would look around and say, How awful! Yes, the town was changing. You couldn't go for a nice Sunday drive anymore, Mrs. Dreher complained, because the countryside was littered with soft drink places, custard stands, hamburger drive-ins. And the town's two biggest mills had moved to North Carolina. Downtown the old Victorian houses, with their eccentric red brick vitality, their towers and porches and porte-cocheres and slate roofs and ironwork trim stood boarded up, abandoned. The New York Central Railroad had cut its timetable—the old Water-Level Route was gone—and only once a day, at 5:20 A.M., did a train stop at Veddersburg. There was a rumor —no one believed it—that "the State" (an ominous-sounding phrase, only slightly less ominous than "the Government," which meant all those crooks in Washington), "the State" (those crooks in Albany) wanted to build an extension of the Thruway straight up Hill Street and the State's right-of-way would take not only the Drehers' Victorian shingle but the Van Duyne house as well. Nobody believed that. They wouldn't tear down a beautiful old house just for a highway. Would they? Why is this allowed? Mrs. Dreher had asked Mrs. Van Duyne. It's called Free Enterprise, Mrs. Van Duyne had said, smiling. In this country, anyone can do anything, almost, as long as they own the property. But what tyranny, Mrs. Dreher had said, to build these ugly things and force the rest of us to look at them! And even this path through the woods, Nell saw, which just a few months ago had been just another boring path through pine and ash and birch and lichen-covered outcroppings of granite, where in summer you could see red-winged blackbirds flit high overhead and that amazing beautiful bird the scarlet tanager, this path was littered with trash: beer cans glittered here and there, broken glass made walking barefoot risky, someone had dumped the back seat of a car into a stand of delicate white wood sorrel and the flowers stood surprised, nodding together, not knowing what to do about it.

Ahead, at the edge of the woods, Nell saw the clearing, last year a farmer's field, now a raw red-brown mud pit crisscrossed with tractor treads like crimps in pastry, and here, at the very beginning of the field, at the top of a satin-barked cherry tree, was their tree house. She stood under it, then softly, twice, called Mina's name. There was no answer, only the waiting silence of woods that know a human is present. Taking hold of the rungs, she hiked herself up. Mina was sitting on the floor of the tree house, silently smoking. Her knees were pulled up as if she had a stomach ache. She was staring out of the tree house window, into the branches.

"Okay," Nell said, "so you forgot."

Mina turned her head slightly toward Nell. Her long, rather thin mouth was pale and her green eyes looked glassy under her dark even brows.

"Hey," Nell said, "what's the matter with you? Are you sick?" She sat cross-legged on the floor and reached for the pack of Pall Malls next to Mina.

Mina shook her head. She was smiling. She cleared her throat, frowned, smiled again.

"Listen," said Nell, "will you please tell me what's going on? Is it some sort of a joke, or what?"

Mina looked away. Her mouth turned up in a one-cornered smile. "I guess it *was* funny."

"What was funny?" said Nell, lighting a cigarette.

"I'll bet she's been coming here all these years."

"Who? To our tree house?"

"Not to the tree house, the field. It's perfect, you see. The Club's right across the road and the edge of the field is sheltered by trees, except for that driveway."

"Perfect for what? What are you talking about?"

"This is it, Nell. This is where she comes. Right here under our very own tree house is where Carrie's mother meets her . . . lovers. And to think that we've never known. Isn't that funny?"

"You mean you saw Mrs. Pettigrew meet someone here?"

"Yeah, isn't that weird? She must have been at the Club and just come over for a quickie."

"Hey, listen."

"It's true, isn't it? That's what it was. They both got into the back seat of his car."

"Maybe they were just talking."

Mina looked at Nell with disgust.

"But I can't believe . . ." Nell said. "At one in the afternoon?"

"Jesus, you're dumb," Mina said.

"But why would she . . . Who was the man?"

Mina carefully put out her cigarette, scrubbing it on the damp boards of the tree house floor. "The man," she said, her smile twisting up on one side, "was simply marvelous. He was . . . dark and short . . . and heavy."

"You didn't recognize him?"

"No."

"What kind of car was he driving?"

"A maroon . . . Cadillac."

"Uh-oh. It must have been Tommy Giordanno's father. You know? The contractor. Maybe that's why they came here, because he owns the field."

Mina shrugged. "Poor Carrie," she said.

"Yeah," said Nell. "Listen. Don't ever tell Carrie. I mean it, Mina. I want you to promise that you'll never tell her. Promise, or I'll never speak to you again."

Mina shrugged. "Why would I tell her?"

"Okay," Nell said, "don't."

They sat in silence. Suddenly, Mina fell forward onto her knees and began pushing things into a pile in the middle of the tree house floor—their dirty paperback books, the old mildewed sofa cushions they used for chairs, the cigar box cache of cigarettes.

"What're you doing?" Nell said.

Mina lit a match and held it to the torn cover of a paperback. The damp paper smoldered and went out.

"Listen, Mina," Nell said, "stop it. You're going to burn it all down."

Mina lit another match and held it to a rope of cotton wadding that fell from a tear in a cushion like a length of intestine. The cotton smoked, then caught. In a moment, the little pile of damp stuff was giving off thick gray smoke, and then one bright flame leaped out of the pile's middle. Nell scrambled out of the tree house, and a second later, Mina slid down, too. They stood in the middle of the hard mud field, watching. The thin black sinuous thread of smoke became a cobra, a column, a cloud. Later, running through the woods, they could hear the steady uphill clang of the Veddersburg No. 1 fire truck, and they looked away from each other as Mrs. Van Duyne came to the kitchen door and said, "Hi, girls, isn't that funny? I thought I smelled smoke. I wonder where the fire could be. Mina, you'd better come in now, I want you to try on your dress one more time. And don't you think you'd better wash your hair? Goodness gracious, Mina, you're fourteen years old. Why, you're all grown up. I shouldn't have to tell you these things."

That night, holding a white tissue-wrapped present in one hand and her long eyelet skirt in the other, Nell came up the front walk of the Van Duyne house for the first time. Was it this that made everything seem so different, coming in the wide fanlit front door to the long hall, or was it the special starched rustle of her petticoat, or having Clay walk in beside her, Clay who tonight wore a white dinner jacket and a cut on his freshly shaven chin and who smelled of after-shave instead of motor oil? It was as if she were a different person and the house were a strange house, one she'd never been in before. There was the fanlit doorway to the living room which as a child—just yesterday—she'd seen as a place, dusty and remote, that they never played in, only passed by. Now, as she came into the living room and laid her gift with the others on the top of the grand piano, Buzz stood up and a strange, fat boy stood up, and even Dr. Van Duyne stood up, which puzzled her. Why were they standing? She glanced at Mrs. Van Duyne, who was sitting at the end of the room, nodding encouragingly. Oh. They were standing for her.

"Now, Nell my dear," Dr. Van Duyne said, smiling down at her over his glasses, "you have a magnificent choice: ginger ale or Pepsi Cola?" He had never used her name before, had never really noticed her, and his noticing her now and something she did not quite understand—a fierce greedy spark that glowed in his eyes—embarrassed her and made her turn to look for Clay.

"You see, Charles," Mrs. Van Duyne said gaily (but what an odd note in her voice—like a threat), "they're almost grown." She, too, looked happy and elegant, and her long pink gown gave a flush to her pale face. The room was a lovely blur—an orange and aqua sunset framed in the front windows between gray silk drapes and the glitter of crystal glasses set out on a tray and the little fire flickering on the hearth. There was a lull like a pause in music and then everyone began talking again, Mrs. Van Duyne to Edwina, who had on earrings so long and heavy they seemed to pull her head down, and Buzz helped his father with the drinks and Nell sat down on the sofa next to Clay, who sat next to the fat boy, John Collier. John sat with his shoulders hunched forward, perhaps because the dinner jacket was too tight—you could see the armhole seams stretch. John had dark hair, brown eyes, little spectacles and a very red face. He smiled but didn't speak. Once he cleared his throat—a giant rumble —but nothing followed it: thunder without rain. Julia came in looking blond and wan, but a tinny mechanical crying began somewhere upstairs and she sighed and went right out again.

"Where's Mina?" Nell asked Clay.

"Still upstairs, I guess," he said, and blew a smoke ring in her direction. "Hey, John? Show Nell how you won the dorm smoke ring contest."

John smiled but kept on looking at the floor. Across the room Mrs. Van Duyne's face lifted and glowed. Mina stood in the doorway. She had on a long slender dress the color of faded violets, with a matching velvet ribbon under the bosom. She stood with her head bent, looking pale and sullen, glanced once at John, bit her lip and looked away. John smiled steadily at the floor. Dr. Van Duyne stood before Nell with a tall cool glass, and as he handed her the drink his fingers unmistakably pressed hers and next to her on the sofa she felt Clay's weight shift uneasily. Someone turned on a lamp. At once the room lost its twilit magic, became yet another strange room, a dim colorless high-ceilinged room full of shabby furniture. There was a large dark stain on the carpet beneath Nell's feet and the gray silk arm of the sofa was greasy and frayed. There were tall shadows in the corners of the room, and despite the little fire, the room was chilly and smelled of damp. She was glad when Mrs. Van Duyne stood up and announced that dinner was ready and they'd best eat now or they'd all be late for the dance.

"Dear God," said Edwina, dropping her wrinkled blue-powdered eyelids, "thank you for what we are about to partake; thank you for our good health and preserving us another year so that we could see our granddaughter's fourteenth birthday. Amen. Rhee?" she said, opening her eyes and laying her ringed hand flat on the dining room table, "Is this another scratch? My poor old Duncan Phyfe. Where do all these scratches come from?"

"From people dragging their rings across the wood," said Mina, down at the other end of the table. The seating arrangement puzzled Nell: Dr. Van Duyne at one end, his mother at the other. Mrs. Van Duyne sat at the corner nearest the kitchen door.

"I wouldn't be so smart, young lady," Edwina said. "Someday this table may be yours."

Mrs. Van Duyne stood up. "I forgot the salad. Start the biscuits, Mina, please. Poor Julia, I don't know how she does it. It seems to me that when one twin gets to sleep, the other wakes up crying."

"Julia's exhausted," Edwina said, "and I'm sure he's no help. As you know, men raised in *that* religion are all brought up to be the Messiah. It must be difficult, taking care of twin babies and a Messiah at the same time. Did I tell you, Charles, that I called Chartwell's office for an appointment?"

"No, Mother," said Dr. Van Duyne. He lifted the cover from a steaming tureen and began to serve the stacked-up plates.

"His nurse was so terribly rude—what's her name, Kranski, Kretski? You'd think these people would make it easier on us and change their names. You know who I mean, don't you, Charles? The little blonde who wears those see-through uniforms. She told me I couldn't have an appointment for six weeks. I explained I was going to Europe and needed a checkup before I left."

"I'll call, Mother," said Dr. Van Duyne.

"I've been so agitated lately, I probably shouldn't even go. I have the feeling I'll never come home alive, Charles, never see you or the children again. Oh, I knew I should have gotten off the Membership Council. Imagine this fellow Giordanno applying for membership. Why do you suppose he's doing it?"

"He says he wants to play golf."

"But the gall, Charles. What makes him think he can get in?"

"He owns all the land on the other side of the highway. We're thinking of putting in some new tennis courts."

"Can't we buy the land from him?"

"He won't sell," said Dr. Van Duyne. "The deal is, he gets in, we get the land."

Mrs. Van Duyne reappeared with the salad bowl and sat down. She laid her napkin across her lap and smiled at John Collier. "You're from West Virginia, John?" she said.

"Ma'am?" John Collier said, looking up. He had been eating so stolidly that beads of perspiration hung on his upper lip. "I'm from Tom's Creek, West Virginia."

"Tom's Creek?" Mrs. Van Duyne said. "Now that's an interesting name. How big is Tom's Creek?"

"You see, Charles," Edwina said, "it's the principle of the thing. If we let in this Giordanno fellow, we'll soon have the Kretskis and Kranskis and God knows what. After all, there is a public golf course."

"On the other hand, Mother," Dr. Van Duyne said, "it might be extremely useful to the Club to have a contractor amongst the membership. Now you take the Club House. There's some talk already of enlarging the dining room so that it might be hired out for weddings and parties. At present it's just too small . . ."

The telephone rang and Mrs. Van Duyne stood up to get it. "It's for you, Charles," she called from the kitchen, came back, sat down, put her napkin across her lap and said, "Now, John, Clay tells me your father's in mining. You must be a very bright boy to come all this way to go to school."

"He's the smartest guy in our class," Clay said, "aren't you Big John? And the star of the wrestling team, right?"

Although the kitchen door was closed they could hear Dr. Van Duyne's voice behind it, at first abrupt and cold, then steadily rising. John Collier raised his head and, spectacles flashing, began to talk in his deep rumbling voice. "My father's a coal miner, not a mine owner, Mrs. Van Duyne. We live in a five-room house and never had electricity until last year. I have five brothers and sisters. There was no work in the mines, so my three older brothers went to North Carolina and got work in a textile mill there. They sent money home, that's why I didn't have to quit school in the sixth grade, the way they did."

Dr. Van Duyne came back to the table, his taut face gray, his eyes flashing. He sat down at the table and asked for the biscuits. Old Mrs. Van Duyne, Edwina, said, "Who was that, Charles?"

"Jud Pettigrew," Dr. Van Duyne said. "This chicken is stone-cold, Henrietta. You know, Buzz, I think you can beat Tim Morgan next week. He's a good net player but his ground strokes are terrible."

"What did Jud want?" old Mrs. Van Duyne asked.

"I hardly know, Mother," said Dr. Van Duyne coldly. "Some damn nonsense about a malpractice case. If you ask me, he's losing his grip. Lately, he's always three sheets to the wind. You see, Buzz, as I look at it, tennis is like surgery, it's all in one's technique. You have to look at it as a series of problems, solve the problem and win, lose and fail."

There was a clink, a silver fork dropped, and down the table, across the candlelight, Nell saw Mina stand up. "I'm not going to the dance, Mother," she said. "I won't wear this awful dress." A lavender blur turned and ran to the dining room doorway. "You're so stupid, Mother," she said. "You're so damn stupid."

She ran up the stairs, and over her head Nell heard a series of doors slam, like a rifle's volley. The dining room walls shook, the chandelier tinkled, and every person at the table simultaneously put out a hand to steady the ringing crystal goblets.

Dr. Van Duyne extracted a watch on a chain from the inside pocket of his dinner jacket, reared back, looked at it over his glasses. "It's getting late. We'd better have dessert. I must say, Henrietta, I find these scenes appalling. I believe we'll have to look at some good boarding schools."

Mrs. Van Duyne stood up. She looked very tired. Her elegant hairdo had melted and hair hung over her forehead and ears in strands.

"I wouldn't go up there," Dr. Van Duyne said.

"Certainly not," said old Mrs. Van Duyne.

She turned from the doorway and instead began clearing the table. A grease spot the size of a fifty-cent piece stained the bosom of her pretty pink dress.

All that week her parents were gone there wasn't much for Nell to do. Alone, she revised her daily schedule, staying up until 2 A.M. to watch late movies on TV, sleeping until ten, playing tennis on the public courts all day, coming home at six for a supper of cold cereal and milk and fruit. In between she read *Great Expectations* and *The Great Gatsby* and wondered at this common theme of Western civilization—how poor little boys want to grow up to be rich so they can marry snobbish little rich girls. She practiced being snobbish but felt her chances at marriage were much diminished—she wasn't rich and her father was loony. Her mother, who didn't believe in paying for long-distance telephone calls, didn't call. Would they cure her father? Mina didn't call and she didn't call Mina. On Thursday it rained all day, a soft heavy summer rain, and she stayed in bed a long time reading, with Taffy sleeping across her feet. Late in the afternoon, when the rain had turned into drizzle, she put on her poncho and walked downtown to see who was around Schuller's Drugstore. As soon as she walked in, she saw Mina sitting in the back booth with Jimmy Dugan and Tommy Giordanno. Tommy was as tall and thin as his father was short and stout, but they had the same leering dark eyes and cocky expression. Now Tommy turned around and gave Nell The Look. Mina was sitting with her face propped on her hand, dreamily smoking.

"Hey, here comes the other one," Tommy said mockingly. "Tell us, Nell, what's it like to be famous?"

"Terrific," Nell said. She boldly slid in next to Jimmy Dugan, who this past year had become shy and sulky with her, and now as she sat down, she could feel him tense and move his body ever so slightly away. She looked at Mina, who smiled at her with half-shut eyes, as if she were looped. Nell hadn't forgiven her for Saturday night, leaving her stuck with John and Clay. Strangely enough, she had ended up liking John, though instead of the Club dance they had gone, the three of them, to a movie in Albany.

"Oh, the burden of fame," Tommy said, rolling his dark eyes.

"Shut up, Tommy," Jimmy said in his flat voice. "Who wants to hear you mouth off all the time?" Jimmy sat hunched over his Coke, holding a cigarette between his thumb and forefinger and looking at it through slit eyes. He had a terrible raw case of acne which did not go well with his red hair.

"Truthfully," Tommy said to Mina with a smile, "what's your old man gonna do now?"

"Do?" Mina said. "He won't do anything."

"You think he'll get clear, huh?"

"He thinks it's an open-and-shut case."

"Oh yeah? So whose fault was it, old Dreher's?"

"I don't have any idea."

"How about you, Dreher?" Tommy asked, looking at her across the table with his dark mocking eyes. "You think your old man's going to get clear?"

"I don't know what you're talking about," Nell said to him.

"You're fooling," Tommy said. "You really don't know, huh?" He grinned, his teeth very straight and white in his tanned face. Giordanno had given his kids the best—even their teeth were expertly taken care of. "What's the matter, don't you read the papers?"

"What papers?" Nell said.

"The good old Veddersburg *Chronicle*," Tommy said.

Mina said sleepily, "The story's in yesterday's *Chronicle*."

"Tell me what's going on, will you, please?"

"Our fathers—your father and mine—are both being sued for medical malpractice."

"The business your father mentioned Saturday night?"

"Umm."

"But he seemed to—brush the whole thing off?"

"Ah yes, that's his style. The impudence of this Anna Gorshak. Anyway, as stated in the *Chronicle* story, Dr. Van Duyne says Potty didn't die because of the operation after his accident, he really died because he'd gotten poor medical treatment all along. From your father."

Nell suddenly felt her eyes blur, and something terrible was happening to her throat—she felt for a moment that she couldn't breathe. The air in the drugstore was stuffy. Old man Schuller had never given in to air conditioning, and instead, high over his head at the back of the store, a huge fan turned its whirring metal blades from right to left, then back again, all the while trailing a fluttering strip of white rag. Underneath the fan, in his high-collared white jacket, old man Schuller pottered about his tinkling bottles and jars and his round bald head reflected a gleam of fluorescent light. Nell fastened on this patch of light now, the way mariners steer their course by a star. Next to her she felt Jimmy Dugan restlessly shift. He said sullenly, "Jesus, I don't know what old lady Gorshak's got so excited about. That kid of hers was no good anyways."

Mina said, yawning, "Legally, that's not much of an argument."

Nell cleared her constricted throat. "Uh—why does your father think that Potty got poor medical attention?"

Mina stubbed out her cigarette. "He thinks the kid should have been institutionalized."

"So the phone call Saturday night . . . so the lawyer is Carrie's father?"

"Mmm," Mina said.

"Hey, Jimmy," Tommy said, "remember when old Doc Lawson cut off my grandfather's leg and he died? Wow, I wonder if he took off the right one."

"Get him dug up, why don'tcha, and find out if you gotta case."

"Not a bad idea," Tommy said. He turned his head to look at Mina. "You think that's a good idea?" His hand slid under the table.

"Jerk," Mina said, "get your hand off my leg."

Nell stood up. "I've got to go."

"Wait a sec," Mina said. "I'll walk to the corner with you."

"Hey," Tommy said to Mina, "don't leave. I was just about to ask you out. I mean, after all, you might not get a chance like this again."

"Hope not," said Mina. She stood up and shook out her khaki poncho. She had white tennis shorts on underneath, and even in the dim light of the drugstore her beautiful long legs shone a rosy tan.

"You know somethin', lady," Tommy said to Mina, "you better watch it. You otta be nice to me, you know. Someday your father might need a job. My father's always lookin' for ditchdiggers."

Tommy sat laughing at them, with his arm thrown across the back of the booth, and Jimmy sat hunched forward, the back of his neck bright red, and at the soda fountain, Ronny Schuller, the druggist's son, looked up at them from under his peaked white cap and instantly looked down and wiped the marble counter.

Outside, gray steam rose from the wet sidewalks. Next door, Burt Murphy in a long white apron, was sweeping the walk in front of Murphy's Fruit Market. Drops of green water rolled off his awning and bounced on the walk. Traffic had picked up, it was almost closing time. Cars swept up and down Main Street, making waves two feet high.

Mina said, "We're leaving tomorrow."

"You are?" Nell said. "For the Cape?"

"Yeah."

"Well then."

"You're not going to camp?"

"No."

"Don't listen to Giordanno, okay? I mean, I don't know what to tell you except that I'm sorry. There's going to be a lot of bad talk."

"Yeah."

"I mean, you know what this town is like."

"Mina, it's all right."

"I'm really sorry about everything."

"It's not your fault, will you stop it?"

"I won't see you again because I'm going right to school from the Cape."

"So you're going away after all? To St. Anne's?"

"Yeah. Well, as a matter of fact, I really want to go. Carrie's going away, too."

"She is? When did you see her?"

"I didn't, Marie Withers told me. At least we're not going to the same school. I wouldn't want to go anywhere Mrs. Miniver goes."

"Mina, don't be mad at Carrie. Things aren't her fault."

"I know," Mina said. "Still. Well. I have to go. Listen, stay well. Don't be too gracious, okay?" She smiled at Nell and then walked away in her forward-sloping walk, the khaki tails of her poncho flapping about her long legs. At the entrance to Jordan's Department Store she abruptly turned.

"Nell," she said, "listen. Someday I'm going to make this up to you."

Nell made a face at her, Mina waved and was gone, and it was years before Nell saw her again.

The Drehers came home on Friday but it took Margarete Dreher a whole day to recover from the trip to New York City. On Saturday she got up, made breakfast, went about her household chores in the usual way, but it was as if she were frozen—she barely talked, just went on dusting the furniture, and in the afternoon, a time when usually she liked to sit in the garden and read, she sat in the living room, smoking and staring at the walls. Dr. Dreher stayed in bed most of the time, and when he was up walking around he was more like an obstacle than a person, something to be moved around or over. He had stopped talking but would, every once in a while, begin to sing broken fragments of song, and then turn his head, look curiously around and stop. At mealtimes he ate slowly, chewing every bite until Nell wanted to scream. And he looked at them both with that same curious look, as if he were in a strange place among strangers.

Saturday night they sat at the table a long while, Mrs. Dreher smoking and Nell looking out at the pale green twilight wishing she had somewhere, anywhere, to go. Dr. Dreher was upstairs in bed, and they could hear through the open windows his crooning song. He was singing the way a three-year-old sings to put himself to sleep.

Mrs. Dreher said, "I suppose I had better tell you about your father."

Nell said nothing. She'd figured out that the news wouldn't be good.

"Your father has a rather rare disease," Mrs. Dreher said. "It has a name—Altzheimer's Disease. It is, more or less, premature senility. There is no hope of recovery."

Nell looked at her mother, whose eyes were so gray and still. "There's nothing that can be done?"

"No."

"But what's the cause of it?"

"Nobody knows." Mrs. Dreher put out her cigarette and sighed. "Nobody knows the cause or the cure. There it is. Now we have to face the next question: what shall we do? For money, I mean. There will be, I hope, some insurance money, but not very much. And I have some money in the bank. The money I made selling houses. In any case, I think we should move."

"Move?" Nell said. "But where to?"

"To New York City, somewhere. I have friends there. Perhaps I can get a job. I don't know what I'm good for. What does a forty-five-year-old woman do who has never worked?"

"You've always worked," Nell said.

"Ah yes, I've cooked and cleaned and helped your father in the office. Besides this, I have all sorts of useless ladylike accomplishments. I am well read, I know Wagner from Sibelius and I have supported the founding of the Veddersburg Art Museum. I wish I could trade some of my culture for a good well-paid job. I look at myself in the mirror and I say, 'Margarete, you're as smart as any plumber or electrician.' But what is there for me to do, Nell? Sell underpants in a department store? Wait on tables?"

Nell stared out of the window. The air outside was pale now, the white light of a summer's day ending. She felt confused. Upstairs, Dr. Dreher was singing tonelessly, "*Du, du, bleibst mir im Herzen,*" over and over again.

"We'll have to stay here until the suit is settled. I don't know, I don't know. Pretty how your friend's father so nicely put it all on us. Of course, every doctor in town will support Van Duyne. Haven't the Van Duynes lived here for two hundred years? Isn't he an Elder in the Church? Isn't he Chief of Surgery? It's not possible, of course, that he could make a mistake. And then there's poor Dreher, of course. He's crazy, he's a foreigner, he's probably a Communist or maybe a Democrat. But you know something, Nell, I don't think your father made any mistake. Not four years ago. If you ask me, Van Duyne made an error in judgment—he's all technique and no heart, a poor combination. You know when that boy died he wouldn't even speak to the woman? Didn't want to miss his tennis game. Couldn't be bothered to say a few words to her. Even a surgeon must occasionally interest himself in the psyche of his patient. A heart error. He's made many of them, even against his own family. A failure of the heart. It's a good thing your father's practice is already closed. Our lives here are over. *Ach,* the whole suit's been cooked up by that lawyer, Pettigrew. He had to find some way to do it."

"Do what?" Nell asked.

"Oh . . ." Mrs. Dreher said, shrugged and stood up. "Make some money. He's in debt up to here"—she swept the edge of her palm across her chin—"and everyone knows it." She jerked the dinner plates off the table and took them to the sink.

They moved toward the end of August. A large silver van with black-shaded red letters backed up their driveway, and all day long three men (one small and stringy and hard-working and two tall and lazy and fat) carried out barrels and rugs and boxes of books and tables covered with dingy pieces of quilting. In the late afternoon, Mrs. Dreher bundled Dr. Dreher into the back seat of the car and Mrs. Dreher, Nell and Taffy got into the front seat. Mrs. Dreher seemed cheerful. "Oh, I've always hated small towns," she said to Nell. "Believe me, there is nothing so exciting as a big city."

Just before twilight, they crossed the Van Duyne Memorial Bridge to the west side of town and the Thruway. Looking out of the window, Nell saw the town stacked up in layers, from the brown river to the old abandoned brick mills, to the brownstone buildings and church spires and the trees of Upper Hill Street. All the windows in town beamed at them, gold from the setting sun.

"Don't look back," said Mrs. Dreher.

"Why not?" Nell asked.

"Because. You'll turn into a pillar of salt."

Dr. Dreher lay in the back seat humming and Taffy panted against Nell's bare arm. Just as they reached the entrance to the Thruway, Nell did look back. On the top of the highest hill she could see the white chimneys of the Van Duynes' house, and she felt a terrible sadness.

"Nell," her mother said, "please give me my cigarettes. You know, Nell, you're a big girl now, almost grown, and so I want to explain something to you about the malpractice suit, about the Pettigrews and the Van Duynes. You see, my dear, things are not always what they seem. Some families are happy and some are not, and all families are different, as are all people, and every person has to find his own way of getting through life. Do you know what impotent means? Well, once upon a time there was a beautiful young girl named Cynthia who married a handsome young lawyer. Pass me the matches, my dear. Here, hold the steering wheel just a second. You see, you are almost grown and that's why you should know some of these things."

FIVE

1.

Humans are creatures of habit. We form habits, they tell us, as time-savers, decision-making shortcuts, but this Wednesday morning when I take my habitual route from office to hospital (a route I have carefully gauged as having less traffic and three fewer lights than the other two possibilities) I encounter a terrible snarl, a huge traffic jam at the corner of Union Avenue and Spruce Street at St. Mary's Church. It's a hot, heavy New Jersey September morning, and in my six-year-old unair-conditioned Volvo, I feel as if I'm in a small, very primitive torture chamber. Where the devil are all these cars coming from? Cars are stacked up three deep at the curb depositing people at the church, the bell tolls—and then I realize that today is Kathy Harrington's funeral and in my mind Kathy laughs the way she did in my office just last week, and this image of Kathy alive is replaced by one of Kathy dead, a blue eye staring up at nothing. I ease past the snarl and creep on toward the hospital. I think that perhaps I should go to the funeral but I am very late and have eight hospital patients to see before I get back to the office: the pressure of things to be done in life makes me somewhat callous toward the ceremonies of death. Still, nothing dissolves death's mysteries. Even after all these years, it's hard to believe that my parents are dead. I wish I could subscribe to some kindly religious fabrication and see them floating over me in white gowns with harps and halos, but this idea makes me smile—wouldn't my mother have hated that? She disliked floppy clothes and had no ear for music, and my father flying? Not very likely—he was afraid of heights. My father once said that he thought there was a sort of electric afterlife —he saw individual souls buzzing through dark blue eternity like the showers of orange sparks fireworks trail on the Fourth of July. My mother would laugh at him and say, "That's just like your father. He has no understanding of nature. We live and we die. That's nature's law."

And when I pull into the doctors' parking lot this humid hot morning, there is still another irritation, another snag in routine: parked in my space (Row C-⚹28) is a bright emerald green Rolls Royce Corniche with a New York license plate. I am left to scrounge, finding a space at last in the back row so close to a metal stanchion that I scratch the whole side of the Volvo's left door and have to climb over the stick shift and get out at the right and performing this maneuver catch the hem of my skirt on the edge of the door, which hem instantly tears. How life is against me this morning! I write the green Rolls a nasty note and leave it under the windshield wiper. Before I even get to the fourth floor, I am aware that my deodorant has quit, and I resort to a splash of Mitsouko in the Ladies' Room.

"About our old gal Peggy," says Ron Carson, an intern in medicine. He is short, baby-faced and blond, and keeps firmly clenched in his teeth a cold pipe. When he lights it, down in the cafeteria or in the lounge, a certain rapid in and out sucking motion makes him resemble an infant of uncertain age. "I'm curious as to why you don't want me to go ahead with peritonoscopy."

This boy loves tests. Given any patient on the floor with the slightest abdominal twinge, he will want to shoot the works.

"Has the lab work come back yet?" I ask.

"Not yet. They're not working weekends anymore."

"Terrific. When did that happen?"

"Notice came through on Friday. Except on an emergency basis, no more tests from Friday at noon until Monday at 6 A.M."

"So then all the weekend lab work gets started on Monday, which means it'll be—uh—this afternoon at the earliest, right?"

"Right."

"Why don't we wait until this afternoon, see what her amylase is going to be."

He is stubborn. "Why?"

"Why? Because there's no sense in doing a painful procedure before the other, simpler tests. Mrs. Peterson's seventy-two. It would be . . . distressing."

He frowns and says, "There's some evidence, in my opinion, that we ought also to do a brain scan."

"A brain scan?" Now I'm really puzzled. I'll bet Ronnie had a big Tinker Toy collection when he was seven or eight.

"In my opinion," (he says humbly) "she might have a liver tumor with metastases to the brain. She's certainly not acting normally. She's been extremely agitated. When I examined her yesterday she was very difficult."

"I see." I do see. Carson has the reputation of being a little bit rough-fingered, and as far as sensitivity to the patient goes, it must be in his shoes, it's certainly not in his hands or his personality. You wonder sometimes how medical schools pick their students. All these kids who get A's in the abstract sciences but have no ability to relate to the living patient. Carson, a Phi Bete, Sigma Xi (who, he once told me, "never bothered" to take any "useless" liberal art courses), is in many human ways—a klutz. Too bad there's no satisfying way of measuring the human qualities of would-be physicians: how, after all, does one objectively determine understanding, dedication, human concern?"

"Listen," I say to Carson, "if you are seventy-two and your husband died last year and your children are far away, well, maybe you've got a right to be a little upset. It's frightening, being ill and alone."

He looks at me condescendingly and turns away to talk to another intern. Poor kid. I've ruined his day. Think of the fun he's going to miss—not getting to play with all that expensive equipment.

I look in on Mrs. Peterson and she does have a wild look. She shrinks under the hospital blanket, her skinny fingers clutching it up to her chin.

"Hi, Mrs. Peterson," I say. "How are you feeling?"

She says nothing. Just stares at me for a moment.

"How was breakfast this morning? Did you eat any of it?"

Silence, but the blanket moves down an inch or so.

"Tell me something, does your tummy hurt? I'm going to press hard here—you let me know if I'm hurting you, all right?" I palpate her liver gently. I know that it's enlarged, but my guess is the primary tumor is in her lung, not her liver. I check her lungs and heart, then cover her up again and pat her arm.

"Nurse tells me you don't like the service around here. You know how it is, Mrs. Peterson. They try hard but there's a lot to do. Do you think you could eat some lunch? Do you have any nausea?"

She slowly moves her head from side to side.

"I'll tell you what we're going to do today. We're going to take some more pictures of your chest. The X rays we've gotten don't give us a complete answer. I'd like some nice clear pictures so we can really see what's going on in there."

She slowly nods, agreeing. Her hair is a wild white tangle.

"Now tell me, is there something bothering you? Dr. Carson says you were very upset yesterday."

She opens her mouth, closes it again. "Glasses," she says in a whisper.

I look on her night stand and see the eyeglasses there and slip them on for her. Her lined face becomes at once more focused, intelligent. I sit down on the edge of the bed and wait. She clears her throat.

"That young man," she says in her frail whispery voice.

"Who's that, Mrs. Peterson?"

"Little blond fellow. Calls me Peggy. Doesn't even know me." There is a look of scorn on her face that I understand. Lying in a hospital bed, dependent on others for your food and toileting, being handled, constantly handled, you lose the feeling that you're anything but flesh. I've seen nurses and doctors, too, who handle patients as if they were sides of beef in a meat locker. I remember once when I was a fourth-year medical student on the ob-gyn ward, sitting in a labor room with a beautiful young woman who was about to have twins. Routinely, the interns and residents on that ward called their patients "Mother," or "Mama." This lady, in the pause between contractions, looked at the intern and said (the look on her face was the same one of scorn), "My name . . . is . . . Mrs. Angotti." Mrs. Peterson had never been Peggy to me. What did Carson know about her, anyway? Did he know that for most of her life she'd supported an alcoholic husband? Quietly, in the way people used to do. Never talked about it. She was the one who really ran Peterson's Lumberyard, had until just recently five people working for her. She was the one who kept the books, made out the orders, checked the deliveries. Little wiry woman with a tongue like a steel thread.

"You mean Dr. Carson? I guess he's got a lot to learn, Mrs. Peterson. He's young. I'll tell you what—if he calls you Peggy, you call him sonny."

A glimmer—very faint—of a smile. "Yesterday . . ." she says in her whisper, then stops. I wait. Her eyes—dim behind the thick glasses—fill with tears. "Yesterday was . . ." She stops again. "My husband died a year ago. Yesterday."

I nod. "I understand. It's lonely, isn't it? Have you talked to your children yet?"

She shakes her head. I sense she is, like so many independent people I've known, deeply ashamed of being ill. "Don't want to bother . . . them."

"But they'll want to know, Mrs. Peterson."

"They . . . have troubles of their own."

"Of course they do. But think how worried they'll be if they try to reach you at home and you're not there. Do you have a friend who would call them for you? A neighbor, perhaps?"

"Agnes," she says, and clears her throat. "Middleton."

"All right," I say, and pat her arm. "I'll get in touch with her. Now if Dr. Carson gets fresh you just give him a good pinch. I know you can do it. I remember you very well, used to buy down at your lumberyard."

Her eyes light up briefly. She smiles. "Agnes," she says in her feathery whisper. "Cheshire Road." I nod and wave and go out the door, thinking now about my next patient, Mrs. McGinnis, but before I have time to avoid him, see bearing down upon me Dr. Artie Papermacher.

Goodness, he does look healthy! He's a lot trimmer than he used to be in medical school, where, as I remember, he had a definite weight problem. Now, twenty pounds lighter, white-haired and with the good ruddy color of an outdoorsman, he looks like the dignified compassionate physician in that old nineteenth century engraving, "The Doctor." But Artie hasn't seen a patient for ten years, and maybe it's a good thing since I remember well how clumsy he used to be—the kind of fumble-fingers you always hoped wouldn't be sharing your table in the laboratory. We used to worry about Artie in those days. What was his medical niche? Surgery—we hoped —was out, so was ob-gyn. Pathology would have been safer for the patient—besides, it offered good pay, nice hours—but when confronted with a microscope and slides, Artie got the most awful headaches. Psychiatry? Although he had a sales-man's smile (his father was one of New York's biggest car dealers) he was a poor listener, as inept in the realm of the psyche as he was among Bunsen burners and retorts. Public Health? Hmm, a possibility, but the pay wasn't very good, and besides, there were all those boring trips to unhealthy India and Africa. Travel would have interfered with his morning tennis game—which, although not naturally very good, has, through rigorous and constant practice, improved a good deal. In fact, Artie, here you are at not quite 10 A.M. with a giant tennis racquet under your arm. Hey, Artie, that's great— it's a "Prince" with a bigger "sweet spot." Now that should help. Artie has been cool to me ever since Vic Bodine and I beat him playing doubles at the hospital's annual medical staff picnic.

"Morning, Nell," he says, giving me the affable grin that has charmed so many generous prospective donors.

I wave briskly and glance at my watch—hint, hint—but this is decidedly not my good morning. Turns out Papermacher has a little something he wants me to do. You see, he has found his niche. For the seventy thousand a year this hospital pays him, he sits (usually between the hours of ten and four) at a desk in an elegantly carpeted room and dreams up projects for doctors like me.

"Just the lady I want to see! Got a minute?"

"Nnn," I mumble apprehensively. What's it going to be this time? Another committee I'm supposed to head up? Another "study" you think "we" should undertake? Or do you want me to pose with a patient? The hospital's new monthly newsletter, put out by our ever growing public relations department, loves cozy doc-patient shots.

"As you know," he says, orotund as ever, "we are about to undertake a study on the feasibility of expanding our ambulatory outpatient care. It's my impression that currently our outpatient facility is woefully underutilized. What do you think, Nell? Am I correct?"

"Been down there lately?" I ask.

"Oh, I've dropped in now and again," he says airily.

"Last week I saw two patients in two hours." Of course

he's correct, he knows he's correct. Those of us who take charge of the outpatient clinic have one main gripe—no one comes in. Summerville is, after all, a more or less middle class town. For physicians who volunteer their time, this clinic is a drag. So what does he mean, expand?

"I'm thinking of putting together a team to factuate my impression."

"Factuate?" I say.

"Let me put it this way," he says in a kindly voice, as if I were a slightly dull child. "As I see it, if we had a bigger, newer facility—completely staffed and equipped—"

"We are now," I interrupt.

"What?" he says.

"We're completely staffed and equipped now," I say. "Artie, I'm not quite clear on what you're saying. Are you telling me that because the hospital doesn't have enough outpatients you want to build a *bigger* outpatient building?"

"You understand," he says modestly, "federal money will be available. A matching program. Ten million Summerville dollars to match ten million federal dollars."

Are the feds really this silly? Giving chic suburban Summerville ten million dollars for nonexistent clinic patients?

"How do you know the money's available?" I ask. Good old trusting Nell—you have been a registered Democrat all your life. You simply can't give up your depression-baby belief in the goodness and high-mindedness of our federal government.

"It's there," Papermacher says smugly, "and we want to see to it that this hospital gets its little piece of the federal pie."

Pie? Hey—that's not pie, it's dough—your dough, my dough. Our tax money, remember? Whatever happened to the sacred trust of government to spend tax money wisely? Forgive me, but I am terribly old-fashioned. I think that what sick people need most is an interested, well-trained doctor, necessary equipment and good nursing care. As for gadgets— all right, I like the new CAT scanner but what about your hyperbaric chamber, my friend? What did it cost this hospital? How many thousands of donated dollars? And the story makes the rounds that it's used once a day—our Director of Public Relations sits inside, inhaling its pure oxygen: he thinks it's going to help his constipation. How about less emphasis on gleaming hardware and more on nursing care? Why is it that in this august institution there is no one to go in and see that Mrs. Peterson eats her breakfast? I remember a time when there were nurses to help those patients too weak to feed themselves. Why is it we spend so much money on administrators, and public relations, and *things* when every physician knows that a good nurse is worth ten gurgling machines? And by the by, Papermacher, the nurses in this hospital are notoriously underpaid.

"Wish I could help," I lie, "but I'm terribly overcommitted."

"I *see*," Artie says coolly. Oh, naughty Nell! Will Papermacher give you a hard time now? Does he sense you're not on his side? You bet he does. And will he win? You bet he will. The trustees of this hospital, who are all earnest, devoted and rich, think he's "simply marvelous, so dedicated, so humane." I go on to my next patient, Mrs. McGinnis, thirty-eight years old and close to death. Her husband, tall, tired, pale, leans over the bed, and although her eyes are closed and she scarcely seems to be breathing, her fingers cling to one button of his coat.

As for Kurtz, he has been moved out of Intensive Care down to the fourth floor, next to Mrs. McGinnis. I drop by his room, and as I stand at the foot of his bed, glancing at his chart, I have the strange feeling he is watching me, but when I raise my eyes his are obviously closed. I had forgotten how well known he is, in medical circles. The house staff have all been coming by to peek in at the great man, and yesterday, in the coffee shop, I heard Ron Carson pompously say, "What a loss to medicine if he dies!" His room is as thick with vegetation as a jungle: gladioli (those stiff vulgar flowers), roses, carnations, potted plants, arrangements of bachelor buttons and zinnias. The nurses have put up his cards and telegrams around the mirror. On the chair next to the bed lies a current copy of *Harper's Bazaar*—odd, that doesn't seem Carrie's type of thing, I'll bet even under the dryer she reads something self-improving, like *Christian Science Monitor*. Kurtz groans, moves his bandaged head a little. His hair has been shaved, of course (oh, how well I remember your hair, that stiff springy pale hair with a part in it like the cut of an ax—and looking at your face—still handsome, you have aged well—I am filled with real pain. My stomach hurts the way it used to when, lurking near a second-story window of Wilder House, I would watch you kissing Mina good night). His hair must by now be a yellowish-white, a salt-and-pepper stubble dots his face. Seen like this, Kurtz looks no better than those derelicts who would sleep in our doorway on East Fifteenth Street. How he hated them. It annoyed him to see them, wobbly and incoherent, flop upon our brownstone stoop. "Garbage," he would say, gritting his teeth as we stepped over them on our way out in the morning. Our marriage broke up over one such, a bum named Potty—hey, no, there's an interesting slip—*Paddy* Moran. Ah yes, it was my father, the good-hearted incompetent, who could not cure Potty, but it was Kurtz, the ambitious technician, who escalated Paddy from this life of pain into the ever after. Kurtz groans again, his eyelids flutter, I quickly leave. Luckily, he's the surgeon's responsibility, not mine. Wouldn't that have made him angry, having me for his physician?

Walking down the hall, I pass a good-looking blond woman whose dress is the green and white of new-minted bills and whose tan is one of those year round tans—August in Maine, October in Hobe Sound, January in Aspen, March in the Islands, June in one of the nicer Hamptons. I do admire her style, the little seed pearls in her ears, her thin white gracefully strapped sandals. I glance over my shoulder at her just as she disappears into Kurtz's room. At the nurses' station I leave some orders, ask casually who Dr. Kurtz's visitor is, as he's still restricted to family. Sarah Ennis looks up, gives me her steely-eyed stare and says dryly, "That's his sister." His sister? I smile at Sarah and nod and ask her for Scotch Tape for my hem, and downstairs in the doctors' parking lot, the emerald green Rolls is still in my parking space.

"I can't believe it, I can't believe it. Isn't it marvelous, Nell? He's going to be all right. I knew it, I knew it all along!" Carrie's radiant face meets me at my door. "I called the hospital from Ellerton this morning. They said he woke up at six and that he can *talk*. And he can *see*, he's not going to be blind, Nell. He's going to be all right." She flops into a chair, an exploding star. She has had her hair done—it is piled up in a high lacquered twist—and she has on a pretty green and white print dress that she tells me happily Dick picked out for her. In celebration, she has bought Chinese food for our supper and left it right in its white waxed containers on the hot-tray in the kitchen. We chatter to each other, getting out plates and forks, putting the kettle on for tea. I try to match her gaiety but I'm uneasy, and when the doorbell rings —at this hour? I never have callers—feel apprehensive. A tall, blond young man in jeans and aviator glasses asks me in a deep voice if Mrs. Kurtz is here, he is John Tremblay, Kathy Harrington's fiancé.

When he removes the glasses, wearily, sitting down, he looks bad. Around the eyes his skin is brown, as if somebody's socked him. He has funny dry rough gold skin which looks blotched instead of freckled. His accent is Southwestern, but we don't go into origins. He sits bent forward as if he had a stomach pain, dangling the glasses between his very long, skinny legs, reminding me of the gardener's friend, the praying mantis. He's come, he says, to see Mrs. Kurtz. He had called her at home, in Ellerton, and found out she was staying right here in Summerville. There is a pause. Carrie's expression is shocked, her eyes look frozen and I feel wary, wondering what he wants. Is he going to say, that son-of-a-bitch, your husband, killed my girl?

He says, after clearing his throat, "Miz Kurtz, I just wanted you to know what happened on Saturday. There was some talk at the hospital Sunday, and I figured, the way it got written up in the local papers, it looked funny to some people and might seem strange to you." He clears his throat again. He tells us in deep reverent tones (he is a resident in medicine at Dick's hospital) what a great man Dr. Kurtz is. He's been working under Dr. Kurtz since last July and he, Kurtz, is not only a great scientist but a real humanitarian. Always going out of his way, etc. Thought nothing, for example, of driving Kathy home, a whole hour out of his way because she was sick and he, John, was worried about her. He was on duty that night and couldn't get off, so Dr. Kurtz, who was leaving for his house in Ellerton, New Jersey, kindly offered to take her home.

A pause. Carrie, lips trembling, says, "Thank you so much, Dr. Tremblay, for coming here. To tell me this now, when you . . ."

He makes a gesture—his long narrow golden hands open up and then fall. The aviator glasses drop on the rug. He scoops them up, stands. "Just thought you ought to know," he says. "I hear Dr. Kurtz is out of coma."

"Yes," Carrie says, "yes."

She looks awful, as if he'd brought her bad news instead of good. We see him to the door and go back to the kitchen. The Chinese food, pork and water chestnuts in a shiny brown sauce, pink shrimp and pea pods in a white sauce, seems, despite the hot-tray, cold and repellent. We sit down at the counter and look at it.

"I don't believe I'm hungry," Carrie says. Her celebratory look is gone, she's just aged ten years. "I don't know why, I'm suddenly exhausted. I guess I'll go to bed."

I suppose she's feeling bad for Dr. Tremblay, but perhaps

there's more to it than that. Anyway, her reaction strikes me as wrong. I take a bath and get into bed, and then suddenly sit straight up and start dialing Jack's number. No answer. I wait five minutes and try again. I dial at least ten times and then sit there with the light on, staring at the wall. What is wrong with me? I am suddenly so lonely for Jack, his solid warm body and the way he listens, the attentive *warmth* of his listening. What the hell is wrong with me, anyway? I've spent all these years building up mental muscles, training myself like a gymnast, honing skills and professional competence so I could function alone—Nell Dreher Kurtz Calverson, who doesn't have anybody and doesn't need anybody, and I am lonely, lonely, lonely for Jack.

Six months after I met Jack Shaughnessy, he made me his first proposition. He called the Sunday morning after Christmas and asked if I would like to go on an architectural tour of New York City. I thought he had in mind one of those tours led by a lady in stout walking shoes, horn-rimmed glasses and a clipboard, but instead we took death-defying Route 22 toward Manhattan, and then before I'd had time to gasp: Stop! we headed right into the glossy bowels of the Queens Midtown Tunnel.

"Wait a minute," I said, "wait just one minute, here. Why are we going to Queens?"

"What?" he said with an air of sweet innocence.

"Queens," I said. "Why are we going to Queens? I spent the worst years of my life in Queens."

"Look at it this way," he said, "this will be a good review. You'll see how far you've come."

"Okay, but why, Jack? I mean, what's there to do in Queens?"

"Just for fun," he said, "I'm about to give you the grand tour of all the Shaughnessy homes. You know? Fill you in on my past. Queens is what I'd write a novel about if I weren't so busy pushing feminine hygiene."

Presently, he was employed (temporarily, he claimed) as a PR person for a firm that made personal products.

"The fucking alimony," he said, "the fucking child support. And what the hell do I get out of this deal? I tell you what I get, I get to write out checks. Yesterday, when I went up for my day with the kids, they weren't even there. She says, 'Oh, gee, Laura's at the orthodontist.' I say, 'How come today?' 'It's so hard to get an appointment,' she says. 'His time is so valuable.' And then when Tim finally appears and we head out for lunch all he talks about is Hank. Hank and his boat."

"You see," I said, "there's Hank. Maybe he'll marry her."

"Hell no," he said. "Hank's got four kids of his own. And even if he did . . ." he said, and then was silent.

"What?" I said.

"Christ, this Hank is a jerk," he blurted. "I don't want my kids brought up by some jerk. Jesus. If I could write one good novel."

"Every Irishman's dream," I said. "But listen. Forget Queens. Nobody wants to read about Queens. Everybody wants to get out of it."

"Not my family," he said. "They love Queens."

"Your family?" I said, beginning to get suspicious.

He had on fur-lined driving gloves, a bulky knit Irish sweater which made him look paunchier than usual, and his face above the turtleneck was despite the loud stale breath of the car heater, purplish red with cold. He began to look gloomy. "I promised Ma we'd be out for dinner. It's the annual—uh—family get-together."

"Damn you," I said. "You could've told me. I'd have put on a clean pair of jeans."

"They won't care," he said.

"I bet," I said.

"Yeah," he said. And already that familiar Queens depression was beginning to settle in. Now under a brittle blue sky, we were galumphing down the Long Island Expressway, hitting every ice-capped pothole, caroming around lost fenders, tires, dead cats and those automobiles full of Puerto Rican children that always seem to have flat tires on Sunday, with a father in a car coat and pink shirt standing there looking helpless while aunts and wives and mothers, all in earrings, lean out of the windows, shouting instructions in Spanish. Cemeteries to the left of us, sausage factories to the right, straight ahead, that eternal Queens landmark, three giant gas tanks painted bright blue, and in between, millions of scrunched-up houses full of people. I began to experience a certain difficulty breathing.

I had loathed living in Queens. Gray days at Grover Cleveland High School, grayer days at home, first in a small house and then a series of apartments that dwindled in size like the boxes of a Chinese puzzle. Those endless look-alike Queens streets that seemed to me a terrible maze, one you could never get out of. The deadness of Queens life, quintessentially small-minded and narrow, without the happier features of small town life. There were kids I met in high school who had never been to Manhattan! There were kids I met who would meet and marry and live forever in good old crowded, potholed, moribund Queens, with all the pains of city life (no space, no grass) and none of the amenities. For three awful years, while my father declined and my mother gallantly moved us around, I plotted my escape. I would go away to college—somewhere, anywhere I could get a scholarship.

Jack's tour started on Seneca Avenue in Ridgewood, Queens, just four blocks, it turned out, from one of the five places the Drehers had lived. *His* first home had been a four-room cold water flat over a butcher shop and his first memory —his mother holding him up to the window to see the bright red trolley go by. Remember, he said with feigned enthusiasm, the sparks at the cable? And putting pennies down on the trolley tracks? Yeah, yeah, yeaah, I returned, slipping easily into the lingo of the region and knowing now that the main purpose of this tour was a stall: Jack didn't want to visit with his folks any more than I did. On to Shaughnessy abodes in Maspeth, Glendale, Elmhurst. When Jack's father, a policeman, had made sergeant, the Shaughnessy family odyssey had ended successfully in Rego Park, in a one-family house with two trees out back and one out front, a garage, a picnic table, a portable barbecue. And that, too, was only four blocks from my mother's last apartment in Rego Park (the Drehers as restless a family as the Shaughnessys, only on the opposite downward route), a one-bedroom apartment where my mother lived for six years after my father died, and then died herself of a heart attack. Three months after she died, I had married Jim Calverson.

Then, under that same bright windswept sky, we sped farther out on the Expressway to northern Queens, to the little mint green split level that the "kids" had chipped in to buy for Ma and Pa Shaughnessy.

"This is Patrick," Jack said jovially, "and here's Sean and Maura and Molly, Bobby's kids, and the twins over there, Tim and Tom, are Ed's, and Ed's youngest two are downstairs, I guess. Patty, where the hell are your kids? I haven't seen any of them for three years now. And look at you, all dressed up like Betty Ford." Jack, too, had slipped into the speech rhythms of his past and a role I hadn't yet seen him in: Shaughnessy Clansman. He was kind and avuncular, hugged all the kids, distributed gifts with a sly smile, joked with his mother, drank with his father, introduced me to all as his fiancée and bragged on (as we used to say in Queens) my face, figure, intelligence, and glossed over lightly—there was only a minimal silence—the fact that I wasn't Catholic. Oh well. Who cared? It wasn't as if he were a kid anymore and his divorce, though it lay like a stone in his mother's throat (her words), was over and done with and it was good to see Jack with a girl smart enough to watch out for her son. Jack's two older brothers were policemen—black-haired, blue-jawed Bobby, with a paunch bigger than Jack's, and tall, skinny, red-haired Arthur, who had a dour, pinched face like Jack's mother. Patty, Jack's younger sister, blond and stout, was with her husband—a slick-haired, red-faced banker named O'Hare who had the bored restless air of a man who's giving up at least two important cocktail parties to spend the day with his wife's folks. She, Patty, was beautifully dressed, but her stiff blond hair already looked slightly askew and her pale blank eyes had already turned glassy and her red-lacquered fingernails stayed wrapped around a tumbler full of scotch that was emptied so fast it always seemed full. Downstairs, in the plywood-paneled family room, the walls surged and bulged with kids, TV, Ping-Pong; the blue lights on the white plastic Christmas tree went on and off and on, and Patty and I kicked off our shoes and curled up on the Naugahyde sofa for a heart-to-heart.

"He's a nice man, Jack is," she said, "always was my favorite brother, I don't know why. Only he needs settling down. It's good to be married, after all, everyone needs a helpmeet. God wants us to marry and have children and love each other. I have five wonderful children—Pete's playing hockey at the Club and Meegan's out riding—oh, it's wonderful being married and having a family, could I ask you something personal, Nell, your being an MD and all, what does it mean when your husband don't sleep with you no more, it's been two years, sometimes I feel like I'll go stark mad."

Card tables were set up in the living room for the kids, adults ate in the dining area: instant mashed potatoes, carrots cooked right in little plastic pouches, a turkey that fell into dry brown threads when poked with a fork and chunks of Jane Parker fruit cake for dessert. Presents followed dinner, and at eight, clobbered blubbering Patty was led out the door by hearty, iron-eyed Martin O'Hare.

"She's on the sauce again," Bobby muttered redundantly to Art. "What in hell is wrong with the woman? Nice kids, a beautiful home, all that dough."

And Jack? My Irish maverick? His moods described an arc from glum to jolly, back down to glum again. At the last, I found him downstairs, in the plywood-paneled basement, slightly plastered, sitting in his dad's Barcalounger in front of the new color TV, his brothers' kids swarming all around. I drove us back to Manhattan. I knew what was wrong. His ex-wife was in Hartford with her family. He was missing his kids.

"Why not?" he asked. He was lying on his back looking up at the ceiling, his hands linked under his head. I played with the tuft of orange hair in his armpit, idly making spit curls.

"Shush," I said. "We'll talk about it later."

"Why not?" he asked again. "Talk now."

"It's the Season," I said. "'Tis the Season to be moony. At Christmas, everyone wants an instant family."

Jack's apartment that night was a real bachelor's place, dishes in the sink, Sunday papers strewn about as if to train an invisible pet. We had made love on his unmade Simmons, which I suspected he had left unmade for just that reason: it's so hard to grapple with a hide-a-bed when you're hot with passion.

"What's the matter?" he said. "Don't you know I love you?"

I slid farther under his crumpled gray sheet. "Uh-huh."

"You're alone, I'm alone. We love each other. We get along. We never fight. Have we ever fought?"

"Only sometimes."

"Men and women were meant to be together."

"My, that sounds familiar. I think I've heard that just lately."

"It's not original."

"You Shaughnessys are big on helpmeets."

"Yeah? Like who?"

"Like your sister, Patty."

"Jesus, poor Pat. She had to go and marry that prick O'Hare. I saw him one night in Michael's Pub with a babe. I

wanted to go punch his bloody face in. Look at her, she's a
zombie."

"Maybe it's not all his fault."

"He sticks her out there in lotus land with the five kids and
three cars and two horses and she's scared to death, poor kid.
She's in over her head."

"He thinks he's done her a favor."

"So you're worried, huh? Think I'll stick you in lotus
land?"

"Fat chance."

"The point is, wouldn't you rather live in New York?"

"Why?"

"Because if we got married it would be nice to live together. In the same place. I mean, we could start out here, in
this apartment, and then find something bigger. A brownstone maybe, with a little yard out back. Wouldn't you like
that?"

Jack's radiators began to knock, the steam heat came
on with a sizzle and clang, and mimicking it, I was suddenly
angry. I sat up, wrapping my arms around my knees.

"What's the matter?" Jack said.

"Dammit," I said.

"What?"

"Wouldn't it be easier for you to move to New Jersey?"

There was a silence. "New Jersey?" he said.

"Look," I said, trying to be patient, "I've spent years building up a medical practice. Have you ever asked yourself what
it was like when I started out? Well, I'll tell you what it was
like. I'd get called out for emergencies and nothing else. At
first, the men would sort of—well—smile but the women, the
women came right out and asked me why I hadn't gone into
obstetrics or pediatrics. It's taken a long time, Jack. Now I've
got patients who trust me and count on me. Don't you see
what you're asking me to do?"

Silence. And then he sighed. "You don't want to get married."

"I *can't* move to New York City."

There was a sound behind me, a stifled groan, a tingle of bedsprings as Jack turned over and buried his head in his pillow. Was he going to say it? Okay, I'll move out to New Jersey? He said, "If you won't, you won't."

"God," I said, getting out of bed, "I might have known. You guys are all alike. Oh, you want all the comforts of a family, but only on your terms, right? Only at your convenience, right? Why, it certainly would make it easier for you, wouldn't it? Having me work to pay for your alimony? I give up. You men are all nuts." I dressed and left, slamming his doors on the way out.

Later that week I got a meliorating letter from Jack which started off: "This seems to be an impasse. You won't work [*won't work!*] in New York and I can't live in New Jersey. Maybe I should explain to you how New Jersey affects me. A terrible drowsiness overcomes me as I head west on Route 22. By the time I've reached Summerville, I am totally under the spell of grass and trees. Lassitude sets in. It's as if I'd been bitten by a tsetse fly. Small town life bores me, particularly suburban New Jersey life, with its odor of upper middle classness, churches, schools, homes, grass, the PTA, Republicanism, country clubs, the Junior League and everything else I am indifferent to, find trivial and small. It's not that I would mind being a fish out of water in Summerville, indeed, I would relish it—it's just that I can't seem to stay awake out of the city. I need a certain amount of grit and bad air to keep going. Writers, unlike doctors, are self-propelled and my propellers need a higher octane fuel than that provided by slumbrous Summerville."

So we went on seeing each other weekends and holidays only, which was more or less satisfactory, all things considered. It wasn't that I didn't understand Jack, I was just too tired to start up again somewhere else. For Jack, moving from Queens to Manhattan was like, say, leaving Veddersburg. Manhattan is a paradox, after all. Stripped of your old associations—your unattractive childhood, your humdrum family and their boring friends, stripped of your roots, you are free to be the you you think you are. At eighteen, Jack had moved from small town Queens to big city Columbia College, just as one bright, very clear September morning I packed a bag and took a train from Grand Central Station to Northampton, Massachusetts. I took a cab—my first one—to the dormitory, thinking all the while how handsome my new suit was and how well I looked and how glad I was that no one at Smith College knew anything about me—my lack of money, or social standing or anything but intense ambition. Cool, good-looking Nell Dreher got out of the cab. The driver carried my bag up the stone steps. As I turned to tip him, I saw at the door opposite mine, our dormitory's brick and ivy twin, a tall, thin, round-shouldered girl with dark blond hair who, as she turned to look over her shoulder at me, said, "Nell! So there you are. We've been looking all over for you. I saw your name in the freshman directory. Come say hello to Mother before she leaves. She's been dying to see you."

She smiled. Mina was more beautiful than I'd remembered and already well known on campus—*The Atlantic Monthly* had just published two of her poems.

SIX

1.

Every fall at Smith on a particularly bright blue October day, the chapel bells are rung, classes are canceled, students are expected to hike or climb—it is Mountain Day. On her fourth Mountain Day, in her senior year at Smith, Nell heard the bells and simply turned over to sleep, but through the wall— covered by paper that resembled a layer of cooked and dried oatmeal—came a series of thuds and thumps, then a ringing crash and an exasperated curse: Margie Dyer, the world's clumsiest junior, was preparing for yet another hopeful march on Amherst. It was a mystery to Nell how a girl so thin could make so much noise. Margie seemed to live in one of those old-time black and white silent films in which everything was precariously poised—ladders swayed, buckets of paint tilted, soup kettles teetered on the very edge of any stove. When Margie was around you mentally covered your ears with your hands. Her love life, unfortunately, was just as uncertain and noisy. She was always loudly in love—groans, squeals of rapture, rhapsodic sighs—"This is it, Nell, this is really *it*." Across the hall, Connie Boguslavsky (Russian emigré father, Boston Peabody-type mother) and Sadie Arekian (New York City Armenian) would no doubt be strapping on their equipment for a hike:

"Hey, Con, do you have the first aid kit?"

"No, I thought you had it."

"No, I have the camera, the binoculars, the Petersen guides and the canteen . . ."

Two doors down, Linda Lou Atkins, freshly steamed and pink out of the shower, was strapping on her equipment, too. Stark-naked and humming, with one long foot balanced on the edge of the toilet seat, she was, no doubt, popping in her diaphragm. She went from one bed to the next (showering in between) with the grace and speed of the goddess Diana, and her hunting trail was littered with the mutilated souls of her victims. She was from Texas, a tall, tawny girl whose strong white teeth protruded just enough to be charming. It was said that she got through Smith (straight A's and B's) by sleeping with professors. She affected a casual outdoorsy sort of sexiness and had never yet been discovered reading a book. How were we to know that in a year she'd be making eighty thousand dollars per and that her face, shoulders, bosom and legs would be looking at us from *Vogue, Harper's Bazaar* and *Glamour?* Next to Linda lived Marge Knutson, a square, somber-faced, dark-haired lady with square dark-framed eyeglasses. Marge was from Minnesota; she never smiled, and talked ve-ry slow-ly and dee-stinctly and was majoring in psychology. She was a behaviorist, and spent a lot of time in a starched white lab coat with a clipboard, a row of colored ball-point pens (blue, black, red) clipped to her lab coat pocket. Somehow it was hard to argue with Marge, sort of like arguing with Karl Marx or Adolf Hitler. The logic of hormones or history, or whatever, always seemed to be on Marge's side.

At half past nine, still in her robe and slippers, Nell drifted downstairs to the mailboxes and found two letters, one from her mother (sigh), the other from Clay Van Duyne. She took the letters back upstairs and sat down at her desk near the window full of golden maple leaves. It was painful to read her mother's letters. Trapped in a small apartment with her sick husband, Mrs. Dreher hardly ever got out. Sometimes a kind neighbor came to stay with Dr. Dreher while Mrs. Dreher went marketing. It was like living with a demanding infant, one who was brain-damaged and slowly dying. Only occasionally now did Dr. Dreher get out of bed. Most of the time he lay on his side and stared at the wall. He had to be fed, diapered, and bathed. His position had to be shifted continually so that he wouldn't develop bedsores. He never spoke, but every so often, usually late at night when the rest of the apartment house was fast asleep, he would begin to howl, an eerie, forlorn howling more that of a beast than a man. When these episodes began the police would arrive and take him off to a local municipal hospital, where he was strapped down to a bed in a room with three other senile patients. Since he could not feed himself and the nurses didn't (there were so few of them and so many elderly people), Mrs. Dreher went to the hospital twice a day to feed him.

"And yesterday," Mrs. Dreher wrote to Nell, "although he didn't speak he looked at me so pitifully that I felt as if he were still there, imprisoned but there. Could I tell you this horrible wish that has been plaguing me? That I wish he would die? And would you believe that yesterday I went out and bought myself a new dress? Oh, how I laughed at myself. No one ever sees me, I never go anywhere. What is this urge that I have then, to remain part of the world beyond my window? We live all our lives in hope of change. The dress" (and still Nell enjoyed her mother's sense of irony—that silver-quick switch from melancholia to humor) "is a handsome brown tweed with a brown velvet belt and collar. I don't wear it, I simply look at it whenever I open the closet door."

The letter from Clay was brief, and said that he was coming up on Saturday and he loved her.

Nell dressed slowly, mentally toying with the alternate possibilities of a holiday, knowing that she would probably dissipate the day in idleness, sunbathing, talking, sitting around. She had to meet Mina at one for a final look at what was going into the year's first issue of the literary magazine. Also (mental note), buy shampoo, walk downtown for taffy apple, drop books off at libe. Glorious October weather, the kind of day that is cool at the margins, blue-shadowed, sunny and full in the middle. Pedaling down to Green Street for coffee, she watched her kilt-covered knees rhythmically rise and fall, felt the cold of the metal handlebars. The steeper angles of purple shadow, the sharp clarity of the October light gave the day a kind of stinging sadness. She parked the bike at the rack outside of the library and shouldered her way through the double glass doors. Suddenly, the whole cool lofty gloom of the library descended upon her, the souls of thousands of scholars suspended like ghosts in the darkness above the main desk, a darkness pierced by a dust-rimmed shaft of light from a tiny upper window. A whisper vaulted upwards, stirring the air where those spirits dwelled. Basilovsky's work on Russian manorialism called to her from the carrels. Ambergris of Parma sighed behind his locked case in the rare-book room. Stay, stay and read. Why not? Pure contrariness to want to read on a holiday. Today let's read about agricultural implements in *The Cambridge Economic History*. Gathering the books and bringing them to a table, well lit by the gold-green sunlight coming through the room's long windows, she thought of the pleasures of scholarship—a stack of clean, blue-lined paper, a good pen, quiet. Do this forever? Why not? Strangely, the gears of her mind instantly meshed and she whizzed right along, fascinated by Cistercian monks and their contributions to crop rotation. She wrote pleasurably on the lined paper, copying sentences and whole paragraphs and noting the page numbers. Finishing a description of something that resembled an early attempt at fertilizer, she sighed, put down her pen. The room was empty except for a professor she did not recognize and at the next writing table a young man who sat facing her. He looked up, stared at her for a second, their eyes met and simultaneously dropped. She picked up her pen, he turned a page and they both went on as they'd been before. Except that, for Nell, everything was changed. The pure and solitary pleasure she had taken in the work was interrupted—she felt as if she'd been caught swimming naked. She began the next chapter now, on the plow, but her sulky mind balked, refused to plow on. Moody, it enjoyed performing alone and for her benefit only. She sighed, looked up and so did he. He was thin, light-haired, pale, with harsh strong features and a shadow of blue on his jaw although it was barely noon. His light hair sprang up from his part as if freshly cleft by an ax. He frowned, drew his thick black brows together and underlined something in his book with a ballpoint pen. Nell put *The Cam. Ec. Hist.* back on its shelf. She drew her papers together and stuck them in a notebook. He stood up, too. He was tall, angular and thin and his wrists stuck out of the sleeves of his brown tweed jacket. She walked down the hall to the glass doors at the front of the building, feeling all the while that he was five paces behind her. At the door she paused for a second and a long arm reached out just at the top of her head and pushed open the door, and she did not trust the precision with which she took in the long white hand and bony wrist speckled with black hair.

"Oh, thanks," she said. He nodded but didn't smile, and his cool eyes instantly flicked away. They stood awkwardly for a moment in the sunshine on the library's broad stone step. My name is Nell, she told him silently, what's yours? He had strange, light, gray eyes and he stood with his head turned away from her and then walked lightly down the steps. For a reason she couldn't define, the way he'd simply left annoyed her. Jerk, she muttered, and this made her smile. Midweek frustration. It was hard to do without men for five days in a row. Without men, the campus resembled not a convent but a women's prison. They were all tough, bad-mouthed, lankhaired until Friday night. But Clay would be here on Saturday and he loved her.

Clay Van Duyne wrote her once a week, sent her flowers and funny presents. He was tall, well built, funny, kind and intensely convinced that Nell needed someone—him—to look out for her. Clay had a common sense solution for everything, liked science, never read novels, was bored by poetry and completely unmoved by history or the collection of Matthew Brady Civil War photographs whose shadows and silences made Nell want to cry. String quartets put him to sleep—he liked country Western music. He could fix almost any piece of machinery, would study the thing for a moment: typewriter, toaster, car engine, whatever, and then, delicately, as if the thing were alive, prod it a little and set it in motion. He was a gentle but insistent lover. The most diplomatic of the Van Duyne children, he had grown up mediating between temperamental strong-willed Mina and charming, handsome, self-willed Buzz. He was, of all the children, most like Mrs. Van Duyne, had inherited her light, sympathetic eyes but had a quirky sense of humor all his own.

"You won't love me," he said, "until we go to bed together."

Nell laughed. She thought he was so funny. Why couldn't she love him? "You're certainly very sure of yourself. What are you, some sort of body mechanic?"

"I have a diploma from the A-1 screwing school," he said.

"I don't think I want to do that just yet," Nell said.

"All right," he said agreeably.

"I don't want to get too involved," Nell said teasingly.

"All right," he said. He sat in a chair in the dorm living room with one long leg dangling over the chair's blue brocaded arm. "Let's go somewhere."

"All right," Nell said. "Where?"

"A motel?" You couldn't do anything with Clay but laugh at him. He said, "It's just that everything seems so simple to me and I don't know why you can't see it. I feel in my mind as if this had been planned all along, a long, long time ago, and I'm just hanging around here, waiting for you to see it, too. I remember the first time you came home with Mina— you were, what? ten?—this fat kid in a T-shirt with orange dribbles on it. God, what a mess you were. I knew right then, and waited and waited. And then, finally, we had a date. That dance, you remember? I thought all week about asking you and taking you home afterwards and kissing you in the back seat of the car, and damned if Mina didn't wreck everything. What the hell was she so upset about, do you know?"

Nell shook her head. Meeting Mina again had been like finding a whole new person, not the ten-year-old tomboy or the willful adolescent but an intelligent, graceful friend who had happened just by chance to have known her years before. Their mutual past was more or less irrelevant, and to keep things simple they had an unspoken agreement never to discuss the lawsuit or any of the things that had happened that summer they were fourteen. "I don't know," she lied to Clay, "girls that age are so moody."

"Awful, awful, awful," Mina said as Nell sat down. It was one o'clock. There was no one in the coffee shop except Stu, the lovelorn counterboy and Mina, sitting at a table in the back. Mina held a coffee cup in one hand and her head in the other. The table was littered with manuscripts, the manuscripts littered with cigarette ashes. "Have you read this yet? 'Once More in Elsinore?'

"Is it Shakespeare criticism?" Nell asked.

"It's the story of adultery in Denmark, plot taken from guess where."

Not raising her head, Mina said, "I liked your essay. Guess we'll use it. Here. Read this. I think maybe it's too boring and long."

Before her senior year, Mina had published poetry in five magazines. Reading Mina's poems, Nell felt depressed and elated, the clean black type on the shiny white page like the early morning, blue-shadowed prints of some mysterious animal on fresh snow. True poetry, like love, announces itself first by certain physiological sensations: the hot forehead, the cold hands, the lover's cramp in the gut. Reading Mina's *Marathon* and *Small Town Circus*, she felt a cold air space swell around her heart mixed with a terrible envy-stab in the thorax. Mina had a career, a profession—Nell did not.

Off and on, Nell had considered becoming a professional historian—oh, the quiet and calm of university libraries, but oh, the long dull climb to the top of the PhD mountain, and the way you had to dig your boots into sometimes shaley information. Historical studies seemed unreal when you came right down to it and the styles in interpretation varied as much as the trends in fashion design. Last year it was psycho history and the year before that administrative history and before that economic, and now they were completing a cycle, recognizing once more, as Professor Kingemann had said just the other day, "the value of political history." " 'Old script engravings,'" Nell read now, " 'worn down by fingers of wind that ceaselessly stroked the stones. Walking among these pitted monuments' . . . What's the name of this?" Nell asked, looking up.

"I think maybe, 'Ancestors and Poetry,'" Mina said.

". . . 'she learned to smoke, read *The Story of Menstruation*, eventually fornicated. She was sixteen' . . . Hey," Nell said, "is this true?"

"Only if it's good," said Mina.

". . . 'he was a married man of twenty-three. They lay down on a tombstone in the grass, and afterwards he cried, laying his head on her heart. 'I'm nobody,' he cried, 'nobody.' He died . . .' That's too sentimental," Nell said.

"Okay, 'lives on,'" Mina said, "which in Veddersburg is even worse. Listen to this, will you? Carrie is going to graduate school." Mina was reading a long, badly typed letter. "Just goes to show they'll take anyone these days."

"I thought you and Carrie were friends again."

"We are but she's not the academic type."

"She's an intelligent person, Mina."

"Mmm. Guess she hasn't found the right man yet, nobody as wonderful as Daddy."

"Don't be nasty now. How's Mrs. Pettigrew doing?"

"Mother says it's the most remarkable transition. Ever since she had her breast removed she's Mrs. Wonderful. She floats around town with an angelic smile on her face and volunteers at the hospital for every crummy job. Having cancer has given her a whole new perspective."

"You're dreadful," Nell said.

"But it's true. Don't you see? Now she has an organizing principle all her own. She and Jud have become the most devoted couple, and oh, they're moving to Florida. Funny, isn't it, how women just wait for things to shape their lives, some man to come along, a child, a move, a disease. Clay coming up this weekend?"

"Uh-huh," Nell said.

"It's getting to be a regular thing," Mina said.

"Pretty much," Nell said. "Going to New York?"

Every other Friday, Mina left for New York, and although she never discussed her weekends, was purposefully vague about where she went, whom she saw, Nell knew she was seeing someone she cared for.

"Actually," Mina said, "he's here. In Northampton."

"Well then," Nell said, "that's getting to be pretty regular, too."

"Don't say that, it scares me. I've always hated the idea of regularity—that kind of dumb, external, middle class sort of order. What a waste of life. Look at my mother. She was at the top of her class at Vassar, did you know that? A little farm girl on a scholarship. So, she meets my father, works at some moronic job while he goes to medical school, then settles down to a life of gardening, child rearing and good works. What a bore."

"Maybe that's what she wanted."

"It's what my father wanted for her. It's frightening, the way women lead the lives men choose for them."

"And you won't?" Nell said to tease her. "Suppose you met someone you were crazy about. Wouldn't you want to lead his life?"

Mina leaned her elbow on the table and ran her fingers

through her hair. "I don't know," she said tensely. "Listen, would you do me a favor? I have to go see Mrs. Andrus about my thesis. Tell Dick I'll be at the art libe, will you?"

"Dick?"

"Dick Kurtz, the guy from New York. I told him I'd meet him here, but he's late."

"But I don't know what he looks like."

"He's tall and thin, with blond hair."

"And a mind like a cretin?"

"Oh no," Mina said, standing up and smiling, her green eyes narrowing. She shoved in the chair. "Read some of these manuscripts, will you? Be good. Don't fall in love with Dick, he's charming but has no character." As Mina went out the rattling glass door of the coffee shop she looked back at Nell and smiled, and Nell felt as if she'd been tossed a challenge. How irritating Mina could be. Nell looked at the big round clock over the fountain. Stu the counterboy was leaning against the sink with his long, veined arms folded across his white apron. His head was turned to the window. He was in love with a sophomore from Chicago and there was no chance, no chance at all of her loving him. This is dumb, Nell thought, I'll read one story and leave. The glass door of the coffee shop rattled and slammed. She turned her head. The young man from the library stood in the doorway, frowning. She felt confused, then felt in her gut a pain as if she'd been running too fast and were winded. He went to the counter and ordered coffee, restlessly drumming a quarter between his fingers. She got up—clumsily, she felt—and went to the counter and said, "Pardon me, are you looking for Mina Van Duyne?"

He turned his head and looked at her, neither admitting nor denying it, just waiting.

"Mina asked me to tell you that she's at the art libe."

Stu put down the mug of steaming coffee. "My name's Dick Kurtz," the young man said. He smiled. "Would you like a cup of coffee?"

"But I don't know what to do," Nell said. Golden October Saturday. Clay had packed a picnic lunch and they had pushed their bikes over tree roots and mudbanks, ferns and swampy inlets, following the gloomy green Mill River. Under a nearby scarlet maple, their bicycles leaned together, wheels tentatively touching. Just above them at a bend in the stream—it really was a stream and not a river—sat an old abandoned red brick mill. The mill, Nell thought, must have been built in the 1840's or '50's—its owners had given it a tower like an Italian campanile. Now its chimneys were tumbling in, the windows were broken, the looms and "hands" had long since gone. Nell liked Northampton. Her friends from Lake Forrest and Rye and Summit and other suburban towns found this puzzling. But then, they had never lived in Veddersburg.

"Do about what?" Clay asked lazily. He was lying on the blanket they'd brought, his knees up, his hands laced under his head.

"My life," said Nell. "I really want to do something but I don't know what."

"I know what," he said. "You can marry me."

"And live in Veddersburg?" Nell asked, smiling. "That used to be a dream of mine. I think I did literally dream that once—that I went to live in your house."

"Then make your dreams come true," Clay said. "Actually, there's no chance of that. I'll probably move around a lot. Geologists have to go where there's work. Besides, I can't believe you'd want to live there. Not really."

Nell was silent for a moment, then reached forward and plucked a grass blade. "I don't," she said.

"Who would?" Clay said. "It's a great town for kids, but for grown-ups? You'd hate it—rotating between the Country Club and women's society meetings at the church. Marry me and see the world."

She was silent again. "And do what?" she asked softly.

"What do you mean?" He sat up and looked at her, amused.

"If I marry you, how will I be doing anything different than what I'd do in Veddersburg?"

"You'll have an interesting life, Nell, don't you see that?"

"How?"

"We'd be going—God—everywhere. Saudi Arabia. Iraq."

"Oh Lord," she said, wrinkling her nose. "The *flies*. And all that *sand*. I don't think I'm up to playing 'whither thou goest.'"

He laughed and took her hand. "Okay," he said. "We'll give you veto power. We'll go wherever you want."

She shook her head at him, frowning. "But don't you see— I'll be doing the same thing I'd do in Veddersburg."

He was faintly exasperated. "Nell the Sphinx is talking in riddles. I know you're terribly bright, but I'm not following. Hey. I'm starved. Pass me a sandwich, will you? The ones marked H are ham and the others are roast beef. Is my sister away this weekend?"

"She's here," Nell said, "somewhere on campus. I saw her Wednesday. We were putting the magazine together."

"How is she? All right?"

"Fine. Her friend is here. Dick . . . Kurtz? Is that his name?"

"Yeah. That's getting sort of heavy."

"Seems that way."

"Think they'll be good for each other?"

"I have no idea. I've only just met him."

"He seems"—Clay shrugged—"a little self-centered. Heck, I don't know. I guess it's just the big brother in me. We've all known Dick for years. He dated Carrie for a while, before he dated Mina. He's really a great guy, it's just that I'd like Mina to be—oh, protected, I guess. She puts on that damn cocky act but underneath she needs someone to look out for her."

"She's always seemed so well in control to me."

"It's not a matter of control," Clay said. "I'd just like to see her marry someone who's going to watch out for her. Dick doesn't seem the type."

"Then maybe she'll take care of him."

"Mina couldn't take care of herself, much less anyone else."

"Oh, I think you're wrong there. I think people live up to their challenges. And opportunities. In some ways Mina is very strong."

"And in some ways not," Clay said.

"But that's true of all of us," Nell said, "men and women."

"Suppose so," Clay said, unwrapping his sandwich, "but I think it's a man's job to take care of his family." He dropped his eyes. "I know you don't really like my father, but I think he's done his job. In regard to us—his family."

"Really?" Nell said, a shade sarcastically, a shade dryly.

"Really," Clay said firmly. "He's supported us. Educated us."

Nell looked at him closely. "And what about your mother?" she asked.

"She's done her job, too," Clay said stubbornly, misunderstanding her, whether on purpose or not she couldn't tell.

"You make it sound simple. And grim."

"Doesn't have to be grim. It depends on the people involved. In fact," he suddenly smiled, "it might be fun. I think if we tried it, it could be."

She took a deep breath. "Clay, I think I want to go to graduate school."

"Well then," he said easily, "go. You could probably get a teaching job anywhere. They have American schools you know, even in Saudi Arabia."

Smiling (and why was it she always kept this silly embarrassed smile on her face—as if to negate the earnestness of what she felt?), she said, "But what makes you think I want to teach?"

He took this lightly. "Don't you? What is it you want to do?"

"I'm not sure."

"I thought you wanted to do history."

"Not so much anymore. It seems too removed from life for me. Have you ever read *Disorder and Early Sorrow*?"

Clay grinned. "Probably not."

"It's about a history professor in Germany, living through the inflation of the twenties. He doesn't understand anything around him—everything is changing. He can't understand his children, their friends, the terrible times—and all the while his special interest is the inflation of the sixteenth century. That's what he truly understands. I don't want to be like that —cut off from the life around me."

"Then what is it you want to do? You want to go to graduate school, but you don't know what in." There was a small— very small—thread of sarcasm in Clay's voice. He's right, Nell thought, I sound foolish. But at the back of her mind was something—an image—of what she wanted to be and do. Not in a library. Not in a laboratory.

He yawned. "Pass me a beer, will you? Aren't you going to eat? You have to keep up your strength, you know." She didn't ask, "Why?" But after they had eaten, annoyed as always in October by the yellow jackets that came zeroing in on their food, they lay back on the blanket, drowsy and content, and stared up at the blue sky.

Clay turned on his side and rested his hand on her hip. His kind eyes smiled at her. "You're such a silly girl," he said in a low voice. "Don't you know that you can do anything? I don't care what it is, whatever you want to do is all right with me." She, too, turned on her side and suddenly wanted to touch his cheek—he hadn't shaved that morning and his face was covered with a gold stubble.

"Scratchy," she said, sleepily stroking his face. She didn't move closer, nor did she move away when he tightened his arm around her and put his lips on her mouth.

Sunday at five the autumn afternoon suddenly revealed a hint of what was to come—gray-streaked, pink wintry clouds ended the day, a stiff wind rattled the red and gold maple leaves. Clay was driving back to Yale with three other guys. The car (bought for a hundred dollars from a stationery salesman) was a battered maroon convertible, with a bashed-in left fender and a long tear in the plastic rear window that had been mended with black electrician's tape, making rear vision impossible.

"Be careful," she yelled to Clay, waved good-bye and ran up the steps with an odd feeling of relief.

Inside the dormitory, gears were shifting from weekend to weekday. Tagged suitcases had come back to the front hall. Someone—she couldn't tell who—was already in the telephone booth, sobbing. Con and Sadie went out in jeans, heavy sweaters, laced up L. L. Bean hunting boots, carrying books and flashlights—another long night at the libe. If they continued to dress alike, people would start to talk. Linda Lou came in blown on a gust of wind, her tawny hair flying, swinging her suitcase through the door and shoving it with the toe of her pump.

"Hey, y'all," she said to Nell, "you have a neat weekend?"

"Sure," Nell said.

"Oh, honey," Linda said, all blue eyes and tall tawny length, "so did I, so did I. I met the most darlin' man."

(Later that night, in curlers and flannel robe, she came in

and sat cross-legged on Nell's bed and said—her West Texas eyes first contemplative, then agate-hard—"Sweetie, that boy friend of yours, is he rich?"

And Nell, trying to write a paper at her desk, said, "Clay? No, not very."

"Tell ya somethin'," Linda said. "If there's one thing I want it's money. My daddy went broke—he was a cotton farmer—and then my mother married this oil man? Only he went broke, too." The sweet Southern gal mask was gone now and Nell was relieved. For the first time in four years, Nell really liked her. "I scrubbed and scratched to get out of West Greensville, Texas, and I don't want to go back." Nell loved it, this raw Texas ambition—like finding a pistachio nut in a rainbow-colored slush of ice.)

But at this moment, Linda went on upstairs, bumping her suitcase at every step, and Nell felt the warm weekend aura dissolve, felt irritable, lonely, could not face her room full of this sad, suddenly wintry gray light and decided to go back to the library and read, this time among the overstuffed chairs and green-shaded lamps of the reading room. She settled herself in a corner of her favorite sofa, twitched the metal chain of the startled lamp. Except for Con and Sadie in their adjoining carrels, no one else was around. She read Huizinga slowly, amorously, feeling the thick darkness of the medieval world he described, its terrors—witchcraft, plague, casual slaughter—fully matched by our more modern, technically perfect systems of torture. Every age has its quota of madmen and barbarians, only now we have given them bigger toys to play with. Why was Clay so indifferent to the past? He lived simply, concretely, solidly, day by day; was not unthoughtful, was more observant than she, for example, a better naturalist—and yet for her, every moment was outlined with a kind of fleeting pain, as if she had to incorporate it all, sieve it, absorb it. Was it his calm rather naïve American assurance that tomorrow would arrive and be pretty much the same as today? Perhaps she was tainted by Europeanism, the feeling that catastrophe is just around the corner—this golden moment may be your last and this comfortable old sofa, the warmth of the hissing radiators, the yellow dorm lights scattered in those long black windows, the yellow beam of light upon this page may in an instant turn to rubble, darkness, pain, death. She looked up. Dick Kurtz was standing in front of her, his narrow hands folded over the edges of a thick textbook.

"Mina says I'm to take you out for supper."

"Mina?" she repeated, feeling uneasy.

"She has a date she can't get out of, about some magazine."

"Oh," Nell said.

"How about that Student Center of yours? Hot dogs, Campbell's soup, that sort of thing."

"I . . ."

"Ice cream for dessert." Suddenly Dick smiled, his face so changed it was like watching a storm pass over the face of a mountain. "This is completely ethical. Mina suggested it. She says she wants me to get to know you. Actually, I think she wants to get rid of me, so watch out."

Nell laughed shakily and put on her coat. At the door his long arm shot out again and Nell saw the pale green stripes in his white shirt cuff. The wind had turned sharp and shrill, whipping around them, turning the walk across campus into a game. They had to shout at each other to be heard, and by the time they had reached the Center, Nell felt excited, the way she did before Christmas or a dance or a holiday, and he was talking about his research project and she was listening, not just with her ears but the way a sea animal listens, with her skin and eyes and pores, and he kept looking at her and smiling, his ears bright red from the wind. Over hot dogs and coffee in the pink formica, fluorescent-lit Student Center (a very fat lady in cap and apron at the counter always furtively nibbling, a roll, a brownie crumb, a bit of bread) he talked. He had known the Van Duynes forever, roomed with Buzz at college, been to their place at the Cape, now goes to medical school in New York, wasn't she dating Mina's brother Clay? The thing is, he said, they're such a great family, Dr. Van Duyne is terrific and Mrs. Van Duyne is too and maybe it's because of him—Dr. Van Duyne—that he finally chose medicine. This project he's working on now is so fantastic. He's been writing a paper on a disease called phenylketonuria.

What? said Nell.

Phenyl-keton-uria, Dick said. Ever heard of it? No? It's a fascinating disease, congenital, kids born with it are usually severely retarded, can't walk properly, sort of stagger, often don't talk. Matter of fact, he first heard of the disease years ago, it was something Dr. Van Duyne said once, one summer at the Cape.

Said? asked Nell. About what?

Oh, about a malpractice suit he'd almost been involved in. The local GP just hadn't been too sharp. The kid had been incorrectly diagnosed.

How did he know? Nell asked, feeling her cheeks burn.

That the kid hadn't been properly diagnosed? Well, he (Van Duyne, knew the kid's symptoms and he did some research; he had said in that dry way of his that although he wasn't a pediatrician he could read, and then he called someone he knew, somebody in pediatrics at Albany Medical College. The treatment? Not much except perhaps a strictly regulated diet. Low in something called phenylalanine. You wonder why Van Duyne stayed in Veddersburg. He could have been really well known. I guess, Dick said, you might say I've always looked up to him. He's sort of been my idol. God. Was it nine already? Time to go. Getting a ride back to New York with a fellow at Chapin House. You thinking about medicine?

What? Nell said, startled.

Are you thinking of going to medical school? You seem so interested, Dick said.

The fellow at Chapin House, a tall guy, solid, in scarf and

camel's-hair coat, stood waiting, angrily pounding one gloved
fist into another.

"Let's go, buddy," he said.

Dick shrugged and started to get in the car and then looked
over his shoulder at her and said, "Nell?" but she turned and
walked away. She felt as if she'd known him always, known
his intelligence, his vanity, his utterly transparent charm, his
moodiness, his egocentric ambition. She walked away from
the car, whose red taillights she could see in her mind's eye,
fishtailing out of the black campus. Sharp as a knife the wind
cut through her coat, and she dug her chin down into the
collar and bunched up her fists in her pockets.

A little before ten, Mina knocked on Nell's door. "Did he
find you?" she asked.

Nell half-turned away from the paper she was trying to
write. It had been going poorly anyhow. Lack of concentration. As if the paper had been iced, words skittered, slid off
the page, crashed into scratches and blots. Mina sat down on
Nell's bed. Nell stiffly smiled.

"Sure thing," she said. "We had a gay repast at Davis. Hot
dogs, ice cream, the usual menu. My," she said with heavy
sarcasm, "it was generous of you to let me have him. Don't
you know anyone who likes real food?"

Mina sat rocking backwards, her fingers linked around one
knee. "What do you think?"

"Of what? Of him? Heavens, I don't know. What can you
tell about a person in an hour?"

Mina smiled. "You don't have any impressions?"

"I don't know. He seems . . . intelligent."

"Oh yes, he's very intelligent."

Nell doodled a question mark on her desk blotter and then
looked up at Mina, who was watching her carefully. She
blurted, "He's very vain."

Mina sat up straight, reached absently under her heavy
sweater for the cigarettes she carried in her shirt pocket. She

had an odd masculine way of lighting up, screwing up her eyes as she inhaled. "I just thought I'd get your opinion." She waved out the match. Her face had an unusual look of blankness.

"I suppose," Nell said, carefully now, filling in the curve of the question mark so that it looked like an eye, "to be absolutely truthful, my instinct is not to trust him. He seems to want . . . applause from all sides. I'm sorry. You asked."

Mina shrugged. "You're just saying that he's ambitious. What's wrong with that? Isn't that what every girl wants? An ambitious man to earn money for her?"

"Hey, I think that would be swell."

"Wouldn't it? That standard good middle class sort of marriage? A big house and lots of kiddies and dogs and a garden, of course. You could grow vegetables."

"I thought we were talking about *you*."

"I guess I really wouldn't like that, Nell. What I want to do is live out the life inside my head."

"Why can't you do both? The point is, if you love him—"

"Oh, that's nonsense, you know," Mina said sharply. "Women simply don't—"

"Don't what?" Nell said. "You're avoiding the question. If you love him—do you love him?" Blandly, Nell the actress asked these questions, found the light of her desk lamp suddenly too bright and put her hand up to shield her eyes.

"The hell with you," Mina said. "You sound like the *Ladies' Home Journal*." She stood up and put out her cigarette on the lid of a jar of Nell's cold cream. "Hey, good-bye. Thanks for nothing."

"You're welcome, I'm sure."

"Maybe we can have a lovely double wedding, you and Clay, Dick and I—crossed swords, orange blossoms, the whole stinking works. No. Wait a minute. Here's what we will do. We'll have a house party right after graduation. At the Cape."

"You and Dick, Clay and I?"

"Absolutely. Carrie too. Were you the one who checked out Kapitzsky on the Russian Revolution? The library can't find it."

"Sorry, no."

"Liar. Good night."

"'Night."

Nell looked down at what she had written. None of it made any sense. She was thoroughly bored with the study of history. She looked up at her reflection in the dark window. The objects of the room—bed, bureau, lamp—looked thin and immaterial, as if they had recently died and these were their transparent ghosts. And that brown-haired girl, tapping her lip with her pencil, who was she? The girl sat looking in, floating at window height with a background of black branches tossing and scrabbling against the glass. I don't know what to do, Nell thought.

All over the dormitory it was Sunday night, the dorm echoed with a quiet resigned hum of study, here and there a cough or a sigh, and next door, Margie Dyer was crying again and down the hall the telephone rang and rang and someone opened a door and yelled, "Freshman, for God's sake, freshman!"

Nell felt very tired. She put her head down on her folded arm and closed her eyes. I don't know what to do, she thought. I wish I knew what to do.

4.

In a long-skirted bathing suit, gaudily splashed with wide-eyed purple flowers, Mrs. Van Duyne picked her way down the sandy, rock-strewn slope toward them. She was coming down sideways and everything about her this morning seemed comic—the dirty laceless sneakers she wore on her feet, the large cone-shaped straw hat that tied under her chin with broad blue bands, the pink towel she wore wrapped around her neck like a prize fighter between rounds.

"Dear God," Mina muttered, raising her head, "will you look at that? It must be the menopause that brings out the clown in some women."

They were sunbathing on the little sandy beach. Above them, at the top of the steep slope, the low white clapboard cottage rambled across the grassy brow of the cliff. The Cape Cod house had surprised Nell. Neatly painted on the outside, it was, inside, as indifferently decorated as the Van Duyne house in Veddersburg and gave off the same air (although here at the seaside, more appropriately) of things (scratched wicker chairs, stiff Victorian rockers with frayed plush arms, old braid rugs) that were not especially appreciated but simply used and used and used again until they expired.

"Where did you get that divine bathing suit?" Mina asked as Mrs. Van Duyne arrived, panting, and sat down on a flat rock near the girls.

"Do you like it?" Mrs. Van Duyne said. "I bought it right in Veddersburg, in Jordan's new cruise shop. Imagine Jordan's opening a cruise shop, Nell. It shows you how chic our town's become." A stiff little sea breeze lifted her skirt and dropped it again, as if ashamed at having peeped, and indeed, Mrs. Van Duyne's legs were a sight—long skinny white legs marked with blue veins, purple splotches, red "spiders" on the thighs.

"Actually," Mina said, "maybe a cruise shop's a good idea, now that all our mills have moved south."

"It's sad," said Mrs. Van Duyne. "It's awful to see the town decline this way. Costs are too high, labor's too high, taxes are too high. I guess we've priced ourselves right out of business. Pretty soon though the South will be industrial and prosperous and dull and upstate New York will be run-down and gothic and interesting."

"Mother has a romantic imagination," Mina said to Nell. "She reads lots of novels. I can't imagine anyone finding Veddersburg interesting."

"I've always found Veddersburg interesting," Mrs. Van Duyne said in her pleasant level voice. "Where did the boys go, Mina? I wanted them to go down and get some lobsters for dinner. Did Carrie go into town? What *is* her boy friend's name?"

"Randolph," Mina said in a bored voice. "How could you forget something so inane?"

"He doesn't look like a Randolph," Mrs. Van Duyne said. "He looks like a George. I keep calling him George."

"I think he looks like a Randolph," Mina said. "That skinny neck and that slicked-down hair. And why doesn't he do something about his glasses, get them straightened or something. It's maddening to watch him push them up every two minutes."

"He seems like a nice boy," Mrs. Van Duyne said, "although perhaps a bit overeager."

Mina shrugged and dropped her head on her bent arm and stretched the fingers of her right hand into the brown sand. The diamond on her thin sunburned hand winked and caught fire. Nell sat up and looked away, out to the water, the beautiful blue bay surrounded by a brown ruff of sandy cliffs and dotted with three jade green islands. Dick and Clay were out there somewhere in the old motorboat, *Winnie the Two*. Perhaps she should have gone with them. Mina was in a vicious mood this morning and she, too, was not in great shape. She was conscious of the beautiful setting and trying hard to be happy in it—the lovely blue June weather, the keen smell of salt air, dead fish, rambler roses. She should have been happy, should have had, anyway, a sense of relief now that exams were done and graduation was over. She had even been accepted into medical school. Instead, she'd found the two days here difficult. Once she and Dick had bumped, coming around the corner of the narrow little stairway and they'd both jumped away and scowled. Mina said teasingly, "Nell and Dick don't like each other." Oh, there was too much group living by far. Eating breakfast together and playing tennis together and swimming together and then, at night, too much to drink. Wrapped up in sweat shirts and blankets, they spent the evenings in front of a small bonfire on the beach love-making together, or almost together, only a few feet apart. Why had she come? Dick and Mina three yards away, murmuring to each other in the dark. Hard to watch them together, looking like the perfect picture of a couple in love. The way he hung on Mrs. Van Duyne and deferred to Mina's father, you'd think he was marrying them. Well, he was, of course. She shouldn't have come. She had said to herself, recklessly, why not? She had put off telling Clay the truth although even Mina knew and had said to her one night last winter, "You don't love Clay, do you?" The way we fool ourselves, keep hoping. And this morning, when Mina had screamed at Dick, a crack appeared in the stony shell of Nell's heart. Mina had sat hunched and miserable at the breakfast table. There seemed to be a white nimbus around her, a mood like a dank fog that proclaimed, leave me alone. When Dr. Van Duyne sat down at the table, she had abruptly, rudely even, gotten up and taken her coffee cup out to the sun porch. They'd all ignored her bad mood. Finally, Dick had gone after her, trying to humor her out of it and she had, after a few terse murmurs, screamed at him, "Leave me alone!" and slammed out of the door. From the kitchen window, Nell could see her scrambling down the cliff and a little quiver of secret shameful joy nestled into the crack in Nell's heart. At the table, Mrs. Van Duyne had listened to it all with lifted brows and Dr. Van Duyne had raised his coffee cup to his lips and said, "She has the emotional maturity of a five-year-old."

Mrs. Van Duyne raised cool eyes from the front page of the Boston *Globe*. "I don't think she's one bit immature," she said. Nell was surprised by the belligerence of her tone.

Dr. Van Duyne made a noise in his throat. "Come. She's willful and spoiled and unsettled. God knows, maybe Dick can tame her, I certainly haven't been able to."

"Your idea of maturity, then, is taming? You never applied that principle to Buzz."

"I think she must learn to compromise."

"Why?"

"We all do our share of compromising," Dr. Van Duyne said coldly.

"Really?" said Mrs. Van Duyne. "And have you ever compromised?"

"Yes," he said wearily, "I have." He scanned the sports section of the newspaper then abruptly stood up, so that the chair scraped against the floor. "Where's my green plaid shirt, do you know?" he asked his wife.

"No," Mrs. Van Duyne said. She did not lift her eyes from the newspaper.

"You haven't seen it at all?" Dr. Van Duyne asked with an operating room snap in his voice.

Mrs. Van Duyne raised her head and, looking at her husband with an expression that Nell could clearly define as dislike, said, "No."

A noisy hunting session had ensued all over the rambling house—doors were opened and slammed, drawers yanked and shoved, still Mrs. Van Duyne sat reading her newspaper, occasionally lifting her coffee cup to her pale lips.

Clay had come to the table carrying a bowl of cornflakes. He patted his mother's arm and sat down at her right and said in a low, humorous voice, "What's he mad about?"

Mrs. Van Duyne's face had pulled down into a one-sided smile and she said good-naturedly, "Why, he's looking for something he lost long ago."

Mrs. Van Duyne sighed, hoisted herself up from the flat rock and said from under the slanted shade of the coolie hat, "Mina, your father's out in the new boat. When he comes in, tell him Miss Kretski called."

"Who?" Mina said.

"Dr. Chartwell's nurse," Mrs. Van Duyne said. And again, in these two simple questions and answers, Nell caught a whole suppressed family history, the sarcastic way, for example that Mina had said, "Who?" and the perfectly level way her mother had replied. "I'm just going up the beach to stretch my legs," said Mrs. Van Duyne. "You girls had better cover up, you're both getting awfully burned." And she turned and went off, the purple-flowered bathing skirt ballooning up and falling in the gusty wind.

"It's odd," Nell said to Mina, "I don't remember your mother this way at all. She's turned into a character."

"When you were a child you saw as a child," said Mina. She stood up and walked away, in the other direction. She had on a gray sweat shirt, pushed up to the elbows, and shorts, old jeans cut off at the top of the thigh. As she walked down the beach Nell thought with a twinge of envy that Mina's long legs were too pretty for a poet's, that she should have been a dancer, and then, sad thought, that once long ago, Mrs. Van Duyne's legs must have been pretty, too.

As *Winnie the Two* came putting around the point, Nell

stood on the end of the dock drying herself with a towel. Squinting out toward the broad squat boat—a Boston Whaler with a motor attached—she saw that Clay had his hand on the tiller and that Dick was lying across the prow, a sailor hat pulled down on his face, his hands linked across his chest. The boat bumped the dock, Clay made the boat fast at the mooring pile.

"Did you see your father out there?" she asked him. "There's a message for him."

"He'll be along," said Clay. "He's somewhere behind us. He's having fun with the new toy." Far off around the point, Nell could hear a motorboat being gunned into high and then throttled down into low again. Clay climbed up onto the dock and, picking up an end of her towel, began playfully drying her back.

"Don't," Nell said, "that makes me nervous."

"Does it?" Clay said. "Then there's hope." Nell smiled but pulled away. Dick too had climbed up on the dock and stood politely a few feet off on the other side of her. She glanced at him and then out at the water.

"Look," she said to Clay, "isn't that someone swimming out there?" She raised her hand, shielding her eyes against the sun.

"It's my crazy sister," Clay said. "She likes to walk to the point and swim home."

"How far is it?" Nell said. "Should she be out there alone?"

"It's not that far, a half mile or so. She does it almost every day. Got a match, Dick?"

Dick was standing with his hands in his pants pockets, watching Mina swim in. He seemed both amused and perplexed by Mina and treated her, Nell thought, with guarded solicitude, as if she were an expensive but poorly trained pet. Mina was close enough now so that they could see the flash of her wet arms in the sun and the sideways tilt of her head. She was an exceptionally strong swimmer.

"No," Dick said, "sorry. Don't have any."

"Skip it," Clay said. "I've found some." Cupping his hands, he lit two cigarettes and handed one to Nell. She took the cigarette but frowned, feeling unpleasantly bound by the little gesture.

"Dick and I have a great idea," Clay said. "Tonight why don't we go over to The Albatross?"

"What for?" Nell asked.

"They have a pretty good band," Clay said. "We could"— he closed his eyes and held out his hands, enclosing an invisible partner—"da-da-dee-dum."

"Mina was within shouting distance now, and Nell cupped her hands and yelled to her. "Hurry up, we're going dancing." Mina did not break her rhythm. Her arms flashed in and out of the water, her head dipped and turned. Across the bay, a tiny sailboat came about and a gull swooped low over Mina's head, and from around the point, that perfect sandy beach sheltered by growths of beach plum and a small stand of pines, came the new boat, roaring along, painted a brilliant white with a stripe of aqua trim. It all happened so fast. The boat turned toward the dock. Mina must have heard the motor and not known where to go, how to get out of the way, because she flailed in the water for a second, then turned and began to swim straight into the boat's path, that huge white prow bearing down on her with its high tail of spume behind and Dr. Van Duyne in sunglasses at the wheel. They all began shouting at once. Nell heard herself screaming, "Go back!" and Clay, grabbing Dick by the arm, had jumped into the Whaler and was desperately pulling at the starter string, and then Nell saw, her hands at her face, Dr. Van Duyne's look of horror as he suddenly wrenched the wheel to the right. Her scream—Mina's scream—must have come before the propeller blades passed over her leg, and years later, remembering it, Nell distinctly saw the water red with blood, or perhaps it was the water in the bottom of the Whaler as they brought Mina in. She lay with her head in Dick's lap. Her eyes were closed, her head thrown back so that the long line of her neck seemed especially vulnerable. Clay had torn his shirt into strips and Dick was steering the boat and at the same time instructing Clay in a low urgent voice on how to apply the tourniquet, and in his silent, bobbing boat, Dr. Van Duyne was standing perfectly still, as if he'd been struck into stone.

Gently, they carried her down the dock. The bandaged leg was splotched with a growing blot of blood, and already Mina looked drained, her face gray, her lips purplish, her eyelids blue. Nell moved down the dock with Clay and Dick and was so intent on her task, gently and carefully supporting Mina's back, that she was almost upon them before she saw Mrs. Van Duyne and Carrie standing together on the beach.

That summer Nell went to summer school in New York City. She took organic chemistry, a terrible grind, and when not studying she called Mina or wrote her long letters. She sent her books and silly games and puzzles. On the telephone, Mina joked about her stump and her "peg," but asked Nell not to come up. She was very tired. At the end of the summer, Mina broke off her engagement to Dick. The next spring she went to Europe and Nell did not hear from her again for eight years.

One March night three weeks after Jim Calverson had gone for good (he had left behind his riding boots and half a case of scotch), Nell came home from the hospital to the apartment on East Sixty-fourth Street. She made herself a cup of tea and thought of all the things she had to do. She had to find a place to practice medicine, she had to find a place to live. She sat listlessly at the tiny kitchenette table, smoking. These last three weeks she had not read the daily papers, nor had she opened the mail. She sifted through the letters—they were almost all bills—and sent them spinning toward the kitchen wastebasket. Some fell in, some missed and hit the floor. She would pay the ones that missed. Between a bill from Kauffman's Saddlery Co. and one from Brooks Brothers was a letter from Mina, postmarked Berlin. She asked for money. Mina wrote that she had a child, a little girl two years old. Both she and the little girl had been sick. She had lost her part-time job as a typist and needed money to come home. God, Germany was a cold, dark, dreary place, no wonder the Germans invented Hitler. If only the sun would come out. She was homesick for Veddersburg—the sparkling blue cold of a North American winter, and summer, oh, the ease and beauty of a small town American summer. Perhaps once she and Molly were home she could write again. She had not been able to write. There was no sun at all, only rain and fog. For seventy-eight days straight, there had been no sun.

By the time Nell sat reading the letter, Mina and the child had been dead for two weeks. The little girl had died of viral pneumonia and Mina had killed herself. Nell kept thinking of the phrase in German, *begegnetet Selbstmord, begegnetet Selbstmord*. She had used sleeping pills.

Six months after Mina's death, her first (posthumous) book of poems appeared. The book was published by an American publishing house, although every publisher in New York City had turned down the collection just the year before.

SEVEN

1.

Sometime during the night the temperature drops—in my dreams I feel cold—and this morning when I get up the September morning is painfully crystalline and clear. Forty-five degrees, says the thermometer next to my bedroom window. I put a raincoat on over my nightgown and go out to check the garden. Everything is sparkling and still. I pull up some dead verbena, but the other flowers—marigolds and asters—look still untouched and I feel relieved. I hate to see the garden die in September. Something, a blurred movement, catches my attention and then Carrie's voice says, "It didn't frost last night after all."

She had been gone two days.

She is sitting on the chaise with her legs up and her face lifted to the pale sun, a corduroy jacket over her shoulders for warmth.

I say, startled, "I didn't see you there."

"I've been here for a little while. It's a beautiful day, isn't it?" There is a drag in her voice that I've noticed with kids on drugs or people who are very tired.

"Where've you been, Carrie? We've been looking for you." I knew she hadn't been home. Her daughter Rhee had called from Ellerton with a message: the dog was sick.

"I went for a long drive. I guess I needed to be by myself."

"Rhee called. They had to take Jenny to the vet."

"Poor Jenny. She's getting old." She shivers slightly and frowns. "I'll go home later today. Somehow, I couldn't face it just yet."

"The kids seem to be getting along well. I had a nice talk with your daughter."

"Did you?"

"What's she like? Does she look like Phil?"

"No, not really. She's blond—very fair. She's not a bit like me, I don't think. Phil and I, we've always been very—I don't know, *en rapport*. I understand Phil. Rhee is so—she's very gifted, I suppose, but rebellious."

"Like Mina," I say, then feel I've been tactless. This is, after all, Carrie's child. But surprisingly, Carrie agrees.

"Yes, she is a little like Mina, though I don't know why that should be. I certainly hope she'll change."

"But why?" I say.

"Because I want her to be happy. Mina was so unhappy. Didn't you sense that? That she was an unhappy person?"

"No, I didn't feel that. I thought she was often intensely happy."

"She's buried in Veddersburg. In the old Dutch Reformed Cemetery."

"Is she? How do you know?"

"Because. I drove to Veddersburg yesterday."

I sit down. "What a funny thing to do. Why did you do that?"

"I don't know. I got out on the Garden State and before I knew it, I was on the Thruway and then I just kept going. I can't analyze it myself, really. When the chips are down, go home? Resurrect the past looking for answers? I don't seem to have any answers right now, only questions. For example. Have you ever wondered why all three of us— you, Mina, me—have had relationships with Dick?"

"Of course," I say gently.

"And yet," she says, "we're all so different."

"My relationship with Dick didn't last long."

She smiles. "Maybe mine has lasted too long. Oh, forgive me. I'm just tired. I spent last night in a motel on the highway. I thought the trucks were coming through the walls. I feel disoriented, Nell. I don't know where I'm going to live or what I'm going to do. I won't be able to stay in Ellerton. I feel like a tree that's been hacked off at the roots. Do you know what I thought yesterday? That the kids and I, we'd be a whole lot better off if he had died. There. Now you know the truth. I'm not a nice person, am I?"

Inside the telephone is ringing and I get up to answer it. It is Phil calling from Ellerton. The dog, Jenny, needs an expensive operation and the question is whether to do it or put her to sleep.

When Kurtz and I were first married we lived in a crumbling old brownstone building on East Fifteenth Street, right across from Stuyvesant Square. I loved that apartment. We had lots of room (the whole fourth floor) and a lovely view of the park, its iron gates and white blossoming catalpa trees and kids on roller skates, old people with canes, young mothers pushing strollers, and when it rained, the paving stones of the walks glistened in marvelous colors—amethyst, ocher, garnet. We didn't have much furniture—a Castro convertible in gray tweed upholstery and many bookcases that Dick had built. That first year we were happy. I didn't mind cooking and Dick helped me with cleaning up—we shared most of the work in that apartment. He had a domestic side I hadn't expected, and on Sunday morning before I got up, he made the world's best French toast and would bring it to me on a tray along with the Sunday *Times*. Yes, he could be very sweet, and the truth was, I passionately loved him. We had, at the very beginning, agreed on several points—that we would stay in New York City for internships and residencies and that we would not have children until I was through training, and I guess, not in so many words, only tacitly, we had agreed not to talk about Mina. I knew that Mina had broken off her engagement but—I never admitted this to myself then—it seemed to me that Dick had let her let him go. And what can I say in my defense? That I hadn't pursued him? I hadn't.

That at first I was cool and tried to avoid him? I did, and he avoided me as well. If we met in the hospital elevator or in the halls we nodded and hurried on by. He was three years ahead of me in training so I didn't see him much—just a heart-stopping bit of his white coat as he turned a corner, or his tie flying—it was always the same blue and black striped tie—as he ran for the First Avenue bus. In my third year at medical school, we students began to see patients on the wards, and I remember how (it was December, a real New York City December, silver-cold and rainy) we met our residents on the medicine ward.

" 'Dr.' Dreher," someone said, "this is Dr. Kurtz, the resident on this ward," and he looked up and frowned, his black brows drawing together, and nodded curtly. I thought that he looked too thin and needed a haircut. Later, I was walking home in the rain—I had great black boots on and a scarf pulled tight under my chin—when he simply appeared beside me. I glanced up at him, then looked away. His raincoat collar was turned up but he wore no hat and raindrops glistened in his stiff pale hair. At the corner we crossed the street together and he put his hand on my elbow in that old-fashioned masculine gesture. We climbed the next curb. He stopped and we stood somewhat apart, not looking at each other. The red of the street light lay in a long shimmering patch on the wet black walk. A bus appeared, deposited its babbling human cargo and left in a cloud of exhaust.

He said, "Mrs. Trigorin is a very interesting patient. Did you get a chance to examine her?"

"Yes," I said. "I've never seen lupus before."

"I haven't much either," he said, and then gravely, "Would you like a cup of coffee?"

We had sandwiches for supper and then went to his apartment, a dingy basement one room on East Twenty-fourth Street. It was surprisingly neat. He flopped down into a chair and said, "Are you going to stay?"

I sat down on the edge of his bed, still in my raincoat and scarf. "I'm living with someone," I said.

He shrugged. "Call him," he said, and I did. People in love are brutally selfish. I called Sandy and said that I wouldn't be in and then sat down again.

"You can take off your coat now," he said. I was born or made without any so-called feminine wiles, no coyness or eyelash-batting, and I had wanted him terribly, all these years. Still, I sat there, hunched forward in my wet raincoat, my hands in the raincoat pockets and said it: *I'd like to talk about Mina.* A cold, rather bored look came over his face. He said, "I don't want to discuss it." I sat there as if I were paralyzed.

"Stand up," he said, "and take off your coat. You'll catch cold and we'll be shorthanded on the ward."

I stood up like a great foolish doll and he undid my scarf and the buttons of my coat and hung everything up—he was swift and neat in everything that he did—and then suddenly, looking at me over his shoulder from the door of the closet, he smiled that dazzling smile that seemed like some sort of west wind, to take all my apprehensions and blow them away like dust. Three weeks later we were married.

It wasn't that I didn't know what he was like, it was only that at first I didn't care. Later, not even so very much later, I began to feel uneasy. How charming he was with his superiors, how sweetly he could turn a compliment, how when we were asked to dinner at the lovely East End Avenue apartment of a leading New York gastroenterologist we had a ghastly fight about what *I* should wear, how persistently he pursued the "right" people, how he began to talk about moving uptown and even found an apartment for me to look at, a horrid sequence of three white-walled boxes for too much money but at a "good" address. And then there were his parents, who, for all sorts of complicated reasons, he didn't get along with, but most of all, I guess, because they embarrassed him. Oh my God, were they *arriviste,* but they'd lavished everything on Dickie, their only child. True, his mother was not only pretentious but boring, a fifty-year-old peroxide blonde with a hoarse New Jersey accent and the manners of a retired cocktail waitress. She had, at forty, discovered that the route to social success was on the golf course and she spent all her days, in hand-sewn gloves and British golf shoes, on the driving range. And there was Sam, his father, whom I rather liked. Poor Sam, my heart went out to him, he had made adequate money in a soft-drink delivery concession, but wonder though he was at the office, he was despised at home, where Elinor couldn't forgive him his Jewishness, and his melancholy belch at the dinner table made her blanch. We saw them once, all that first year, and when they arrived one day for a tour of the hospital Dick simply disappeared, leaving me to show them around. So that you see, after a year of living together, I still loved him but I wasn't sure I liked him.

It was the Paddy Moran business that did our marriage in. One beautiful spring Saturday, I walked home from the hospital and I couldn't resist the park. I bought a toasted almond Good Humor and sat down on a bench near the sandpit, where a chubby two-year-old with dimpled knees was pushing a dump truck. A derelict (red face, gray whiskers, dirty checked trousers) sat down at the other end of the bench and crossed his legs. He wore saddle shoes cut out at the toes and no socks. I felt his watery eyes watching me.

"Beautiful day," Paddy said. I nodded severely but kept watching the toddler, who was kneeling now, intently making a rum-rum-rum engine sound. "Pardon me if I'm mistaken," Paddy said. "But your face, now, it's awful familiar." I gave him a wiseacre look—aw, come on, fella—but he smiled blearily and said he was sure he'd seen me at Bellevue Hospital, where only recently he'd had a long sojourn. Oh really? I said. What were you in for? He gave me a lengthy description of his symptoms. He gave me, besides, his views on life, marriage, politics, Britain, poetry. He was sentimental, cynical, uneducated, optimistic and funny, most of all, funny, and four weeks later, he appeared in the emergency room, courtesy of a NYPD car. I knew it was inevitable that he was going to die, in a couple of years, maybe sooner: his liver was as small and knobby and hard as a walnut. But he thought of it all—living—as a sort of game. He had beaten out death four times and wanted another try.

Dick had by this time already decided against private practice. He had a grant for a research project that he hoped would generate yet another grant and eventually a place somewhere prestigious as Professor of Internal Medicine. He had cultivated acquaintances at a medical school farther uptown and knew that they needed an upcoming young hepatologist. I talked to him, of course, about Paddy. He listened carefully and said what I'd hoped he would say, that next time Paddy was in he'd have a look at his liver. Sure enough, not two months later, Paddy was back in the hospital. Did I question the value of the energy and time spent preserving this old drunk? No, not really. You see, I knew one thing about Paddy and it was this: that he enjoyed his life—the best reason I know for preserving it. So we got him out of the coma—I was an intern by this time, he was my patient—and I knew Paddy was going to make it again. Hey, what a great score, Paddy, I said, beating out death five times.

Dick was on call that weekend and had to sleep at the hospital. I went to a movie alone on Saturday night and slept late Sunday morning. I got up, baked a pie, washed out some sweaters, but late in the afternoon I began to feel restless. I tried to read but couldn't, and decided to walk to the hospital and take Dick a piece of pie for supper, and while there, drop by the ward. There, on the ward, no one wanted to deal with me. The RN on the floor was very busy on the telephone and the student nurses looked flustered and Bronstein, the second-year resident, went off to the Men's Room. Paddy was in a coma, far gone, dying.

Bronstein, the resident, reappeared, looking uncomfortable. "Just what seems to be the problem?" he asked, avoiding my eyes. The RN hung up the phone. In that snide way charge nurses have of dealing with interns, she said, "Look on the chart. You'll find all the information."

I had seen the chart, but I wouldn't believe it. Who had ordered R. Kurtz to biopsy my patient?

"Sorry," Bronstein said, and he bit at the skin of a hangnail, "I got overruled. Look at it this way," he said, sucking his finger and frowning. "It's the chain of command. We have to assume they *know*." They? My husband, R. Kurtz, was the senior resident. Dick himself had done that biopsy, stuck that needle into Paddy's swollen liver. He knew, didn't he, that the liver would bleed? And bleed? And bleed? The tissue. Do you see? He wanted a sample of liver tissue. For his project.

And Paddy died at one o'clock that morning.

We didn't split up right away, it was just that I couldn't bear to have him touch me. In truth, maybe the incident only confirmed my deepest feelings about him, but I could no longer bear to have him touch me and a month later he packed up and moved in with a nurse who lived on Third Avenue in a much nicer apartment.

Doctors take risks all the time. Sometimes you risk a month of health against a year of pain. The calculated risk is part of medicine. I thought at first (no, tried to believe) that Dick had had good reasons. It just wasn't so. There is an old rule in medicine that goes back to ancient times—*primum non nocere*—first do no harm. Dick knew that chances were the biopsy could kill him. Maybe this sort of thing happens in medicine more than one likes to admit—there are always ambitious young technicians prone to "heart failures." But I didn't want to be married to one. And what about me? I was Paddy's doctor. His life was my responsibility. Didn't Dick care about me, my feelings, my competence, hard work and professionalism? It occurred to me then that he'd risked it *be-*

cause Paddy was my patient. I was his wife. He assumed my first loyalty would be to him, that I wouldn't "squeal."

There are certain kinds of men in the world—just as there are certain women—who treat marriage as one of the commoner forms of exploitation. I didn't squeal on Dick. Instead, I got a quick divorce. A month after it was final, Dick married Carrie Pettigrew.

"You see, I thought it was Kathy. When I read the thing in the paper, I was—well, I suppose it confirmed what I'd suspected for a long time. After all, he does sleep on the edge of the bed."

Her tone is ironic, and thank God for it. I like that iron in her tone, as well as the humor.

"And then I thought, she's *dead*. That's *it*. You see? I'm not a nice person at all."

"And then Tremblay came by."

"And I knew it wasn't this Kathy but somebody else. Somebody alive."

Still in my raincoat, I am making a pot of coffee. "He's never said anything?"

"No."

"Then how can you be so sure?"

"I did see a woman in his room at the hospital."

"But if he's never said anything . . ."

"Oh, Nell, I'm just a robot, really. He hardly notices me. I walk around the house picking up things and cleaning until I feel like a thing myself. If it weren't for the kids—"

"But, Carrie, you've got a life, too."

"The kids are my life, Nell. You don't understand. I've spent seventeen years with these kids."

"Surely you could get custody."

"And live on what? The ten thousand a year some kindly old judge will award us? I'd rather let Dick have them. Wait. I take that back."

"You know what I'd do first?"

"What?"

"Get a job."

"A job? Doing what, selling underpants in some depart-ment store?"

I have heard this line somewhere before.

"I'd get a job and then I'd talk to Dick."

"It's hopeless," she says.

"Or a marriage counselor, Carrie. I know this sounds ba-nal . . ."

"You see, I still love him," she says. "Some people just go on and on loving, even when there's no hope. I think even when we got married he didn't love me."

"Carrie . . ."

"It's true, Nell. *I* loved him. And I was there. Available."

I smile at her and reach across the counter and put my hand on hers. Her hand is rough and warm, a good mother's hand. "Hey, Carrie-babe," I say, "look at it this way. You're just not a quitter."

I pour two mugs of hot coffee. Thank God for coffee, hot baths, gardens, books, dogs and irony. These are the things of life that keep us sane.

Carrie sighs. "Poor old Jenny," she says. "I hope she makes it."

"I guess I had this idea that Veddersburg would look like home," Carrie says, "but it didn't. The town turned out to be just a collection of buildings. Actually, it was the landscape that got to me, if anything did. The hills and the river. Remember the river when we were kids? It was so busy. There was all kinds of river traffic, barges going up and down. Now the river's just—empty. Nothing on it. The town's so sad. The highway crosses right over Hill Street. Your old house is gone—there's an Exxon station where it used to be. The Van Duynes' house is there but everything around it has changed. Remember how the house used to stand at the very top of the town? Well, the town's crept past it. The new Mrs. Van Duyne sold off the land in back of the house, so now where Mrs. Van Duyne's garden used to be there's an awful shopping mall, an A & P, a pizza place, a laundromat. Downtown looks awful, too. Maybe it always did, I don't know. It's so shabby. Jordan's is gone. There's some sort of discount store there now. The thing you notice most are the loan offices. That seems to be the major business."

"It never was much of a town."

"I guess not. It was home, though." We look at each other and smile.

"Anyway. I went to call on the Van Duynes and there was a new Mrs. Van Duyne. They got divorced quite a long time ago. The new Mrs. Van Duyne is about fifty, I'd say. She had on an aqua pants suit and lots of jewelry. She used to be a nurse. Kretski, she said her name was. I felt sorry for her. He's senile and she takes care of him. He just sits in his wheelchair and mumbles."

"Good," I say. "I never much liked Dr. Van Duyne."

"Didn't you?" she says, surprised. "He was always so kind to me. Anyway, Mary Ann—she asked me to call her that— Mary Ann has done the whole house over. It was startling. She's painted all the walls a flat white and has everything carpeted in bright blue or acid green. In the dining room she's put up dark blue wallpaper with big white flowers. 'The Ancestor'—remember that portrait?—he looks awfully uncomfortable." We smile at each other again. "Oh. And they—the new Mrs. and the Dr.—have twin boys. The boys had just gone back to boarding school. She showed me their pictures. Nice-looking kids, very Polish-looking, somehow—blond with long noses, not a bit like the Van Duynes. Well, I ended up rather liking Mary Ann. I guess she thought she was marrying into the *crème de la crème* and instead got the bottom of the barrel. She's had to go back to work and now more or less supports them."

"Oh, I can't believe that. Why, he must have made lots of money. Where did it all go?"

"I don't know. Not to our Mrs. Van Duyne, that's for certain. Apparently the house and all the furniture never belonged to her, it was all the old lady's—Edwina's. They even paid the old lady rent. All those years, and when Edwina died she left her entire estate to the Veddersburg Garden Club. Now there's a tiny park down near the Presbyterian church. It's called the Edwina Van Duyne Memorial Garden. Workmen dig it up six times a year and plant it with flowers."

"Lord, what a bitch she was!"

"Wasn't she? My mother hated her. Apparently Edwina prevented her from joining the Garden Club. Just plain blackballed her. Mother never forgave her." She pours cream into her coffee.

I say, "Where's our Mrs. Van Duyne? Is she still alive?"

"Oh yes. You remember Van Dam Lane, that little row of houses by the river?"

"Of course. We lived in one when we first came to Veddersburg."

"Did you? I didn't know that. Which one did you live in?"

"Number eight, the one with the red shutters. My mother bought it from Joe Smith, the church sexton. She did it all over and sold it again."

"Isn't that odd? That's where she lives. It's a darling house."

"I'm glad she has something of her own, at long last."

"She doesn't own it, Nell, she rents it. She never had the money to buy it. When they divorced she got a settlement of five thousand dollars. Can you believe it? After thirty years of marriage? Anyway, she took the money and got her teaching degree and was lucky enough to get a job. She's retired now, of course. She seems very happy. She has her church work and clubs, and"—Carrie smiles—"while I was there, she had a gentleman caller. Now, Nell, don't laugh. I think that if I hadn't been there they would have headed right for the bedroom. He's a farmer, a nice old man who lives out by Tom's Ford, somebody she used to know when she was young."

"Why don't they get married?"

"He *is* married. Can you believe it? Our Mrs. Van Duyne, an adulteress? His wife has been sick for years and Rhee goes out and visits her, too."

"Dear God, a golden age *ménage à trois*."

"I don't blame her, do you? Her children are all scattered. Buzz is out in California, he's on wife number three, I gather, and Clay and his wife live in Arizona, and Peter's a marine biologist and lives in Florida. Julia divorced her first husband and lives in Denver, Colorado. Do you know, *she* divorced *him*."

"Who?" I say. "Julia?"

"No," Carrie says. "Our Mrs. Van Duyne divorced *him*.

She said . . . she told me, she'd always meant to do it when the children were grown. I guess . . . well, I was shocked. I'd always thought they were such a happy family. Didn't you think so, too?"

"I suppose, at first. Later I wasn't so sure."

"She's a terribly brave woman. Just thinking of getting divorced at fifty and— Oh. Tommy Giordanno. I knew there was something else I wanted to tell you."

"I'm not sure I want to hear this."

"He's a lawyer now and very looked up to."

"Dear God."

"They've built a huge modern house to the north of Veddersburg and"—Carrie grins—"he's president of the Roaring Brook Club." She stands up and puts her coffee cup in the sink.

Saying good-bye, we are formal with each other. She gets into her station wagon and squints up at me through the rolled-down window.

"Thank you for everything, Nell."

"You're very welcome, Carrie. I really mean it."

"I won't be coming back here."

"I know."

"Don't think badly of me," she says.

"Oh, Carrie," I say, "how could I?"

"There are things you don't understand."

"I know."

"You remember that day at the Cape? When Mina—got hurt? You see, I've always thought that she swam toward the boat."

So here it is at last, this question I've been wanting to ask you, Carrie, and all along you felt it, too. That she swam toward the boat. Not out of confusion, but on purpose. Because, well, she figured she owed me, Carrie, and because she knew I loved Dick and because she was scared of marriage and in some instinctual way, I think, was making sure she'd never have to marry, and maybe because she hated and/or loved her father and wanted him in a blind sort of way to rescue her or maybe instead wanted to injure him. Which she did: Mrs. Van Duyne blamed him for the accident and never forgave him.

"I mean," Carrie says, "swam toward the boat on purpose. Don't look like that, Nell. I know this sounds crazy and maybe it is, but I've always felt she was . . . giving me Dick. I'd dated him first, you see, when I was at boarding school. Then she took him up and—well, I never could compete with Mina. Mina always disliked me, I never knew why. I was such an unhappy kid, Nell. I guess I was just too attached to Mina's mother."

She drove off, I waved. A week later a gold and white box came my way from Saks Fifth Avenue. It was a large silver ice bucket, the kind of thing you send for a wedding gift when you don't really know the couple very well. The card said, "We're both fine. Many thanks. Carrie and Dick." The word fine was underlined.

EIGHT

1.

One Sunday when we had known each other two or three weeks we drove down to Pennsylvania. We were already in love. Knew it at once. We took a picnic lunch, brie and crackers, red wine and fruit, and drove to a little meadow-y park in Bucks County, near the Delaware River. We spread a quilt under a sycamore. I was sitting up cross-legged, he lay on his stomach, head on his folded arms and when he suddenly lifted one gold-brown eye, I laughed.

"What's funny?" Jack asked.

"You. Your eye. It suddenly reminded me . . ."

"Of somebody you used to know," Jack said.

"Not somebody," I said, teasing. "My dog. The dog I had when I was a kid. She used to cock one eye like that."

"Cock, eh?" said Jack. "Interesting. Interesting choice of words."

"You nut. It was a lady dog."

"Still. This explains something."

"What?"

"The way you treat me."

"You think I treat you like a dog? Tush. You're spoiled. I've been much too kind."

"Kindness is as kindness does," he said. He had lifted himself up a little, propped his head on one hand. The other hand, large, blunt-fingered, freckled, was slowly sliding up my leg. Shin. Knee. Thigh. I took it from under my skirt and laid it flat on the quilt.

"Public place," I said.

"Private parts?" he said.

"Very," I said. "Though I do wonder sometimes how many people *you've* loved."

"Ah me," he said, fell over and rolled on his back. His hands lay lightly curved on his chest. "The sadness of my life. Why couldn't she be a nice simple girl who just likes to screw?"

"You'd be bored," I said.

"Try me," he said, smiling slightly. His eyes were closed. A little blue June breeze ruffled the sycamore leaves and cast a shower of sun dots on his freckled face. Freckled eyelids, faintly green-veined.

"Seriously," I said.

"Too many to count," he said. "My mother, my father, my brothers, my sister—"

"Lo, here speaketh pre-Freudian man. I meant women, Jack. Lovers. Did you ever have a male lover?"

"Not yet," he said, "though it may come to that. Would it be too public of me to put my head in your lap?"

I consented. Big heavy red head. I put my arm around his damp neck.

"Was Nancy the only one? Come on, tell me. I need to put your life together."

"So do I," he said. "Mary Agnes. She was the first. First love. I loved her because she never wore underpants. She was an older woman. Six to my five. I'd follow her to the playground and stand at the bottom of the slide, looking up. I loved her with my whole heart."

"What happened to her?"

"Happened? I don't know. She probably went right on underpantless. Then she was sixteen, got pregnant, married, the usual story."

"That was sex, not love."

"Ah no, you're wrong. She had a cloud of curly dark hair and blue eyes and two little rosebuds for mouths."

I laughed, then wanting to shift my position, said accusingly, "Your head is heavy 'cause it's so full of junk."

"Poor head," he said. "Forgive it. It knows not what it does. The proximity of my live mind to your dead ass is somehow confusing."

"It's not dead, merely resting. You know, I knew a boy in medical school who had a weird fantasy. He wanted to make love in the anatomy lab."

Jack opened his eyes. "Saints presarve us, how shocking. Why?"

"Oh, he had this thing about life in death, I don't know. He had some strange rather literary ideas. We didn't, Jack, for heaven's sake."

"Right up there with all the stiffs, eh? Tell me, would he have done it on the floor or right up on a table?"

"We didn't get that far in our discussion."

"No wonder you divorced him."

"Oh, it wasn't him—not Kurtz—it was another boy. A sweet boy, really. His name was Sandy. I met him my first day in medical school. When they pulled the sheet off our cadaver, he fainted. But after that he was fine. He's a psychiatrist now. He never cared much for the blood and guts business of medicine."

"And what did you do?"

"When he fainted?"

"When it came time to dissect the body."

That first day? The terrible smell of formaldehyde. The new light-filled anatomy lab and all of us brand-new medical students, young and looking a little green. Standing four to a table around our draped stiffs. I was scared. Didn't want to fail. Afraid I would puke. "Today, gentlemen," said the professor, "*and* gentle lady, we will work on the thorax." We pulled the wet sheet back. Oscar Lee, his name was, our cadaver. Giant of a black man, skin a blackish purple. Face was squashed-looking, but majestic and sad. The anatomy professor—a small meticulous German—smiling ironically at us. Always that courteous ironic tone. A necessity. Like medical students' awful jokes. Two boys at the next table would play toss with their cadaver's kidneys. Why? Relief of tension, I guess. Must make it into a thing. This body is no longer alive. Make it into a thing, I told myself, and concentrate precisely on what you are doing. The professor's ironic voice.

"Actually," I said, "I liked anatomy. It was interesting. I did find out, though, that pathology wasn't for me. I found out that what I liked about medicine was—well, my relationship with the patient. The live patient."

"It's nice that you're not a ghoul," Jack said.

"It's a balance," I said. "You have to treat the body as a thing in order to treat the person, who is not."

"It's a balance easily forgotten," Jack said.

"Yes, it is," I said. "Sometimes doctors do forget that. Once, when I was a kid, my father was almost involved in a malpractice suit."

"Almost?"

"Oh, it was settled out of court. But I think— I've always thought that the other doctor had forgotten the balance. Technically, he was right. Psychologically, he was wrong. My mother called it a 'heart failure.' She said that the greatest sin of our species was treating people like things. Funny. Later I almost loved his son."

"Whose?"

"What? Oh, the surgeon's."

"Why didn't you?"

"I don't know. Too easy, I guess. He wanted so much to take care of me and I wanted to do something for myself. I'd have ended up like that song in *The King and I*—'protected out of everything I own.' That has to be a balance, too—the caring. I guess I've always swung along from men who need to be cared for to men who want to take care of me."

"Why not have both in one?" Jack said and smiled.

"Yes," I said. "Why not?"

"Besides," Jack said, "we belong together. You're a pill peddler and I'm a word peddler. We peddlers are really wanderers. We carry our security around with us. Did you know, by the way, that Shaughnessy means wanderer, in Gaelic?"

Suddenly, with a blinding sun-flash of cymbals, a shako-hatted girl in white boots and a white skirt high-stepped onto the field and behind her, all carrying their batons at precise angles across their gold-frogged and brass-buttoned chests, came a double line of drum majorettes and then a band, the trombones and trumpets and tubas and French horns all catching the strong June sun. Not more than fifty yards away they marched to something ear-splittingly Sousa.

"My God," said Jack, sitting upright. I started to laugh. I leaned against his shoulder and put my mouth against his warm fuzzy ear.

"Jesus God," he complained, "what a way to torture a man. Will you look at those girls, their legs all flying around like that."

"Hey," I said, "let's go home. Let's go somewhere and make love. I think I'd better take care of you."

Now alone on Sundays (how endless the day is, boring and long), I take long drives. I take 287 down to Pennsylvania or go up the Thruway to the Catskills. It's silent and peaceful driving through the winter countryside, and coming home, I can see the hills with a dark, lacy, upstanding ruffle of bare-branched trees and the pink winter sun setting behind. Today, though, it's snowing and I have a cold. I build a fire in the bedroom fireplace, make a pot of tea and get into bed under a heap of blankets and Kleenex and Sunday papers, and Mina's new book.

Just after Carrie left, I got a letter from Jack. Suddenly, he was in London with a new job and "digs" he was sure I'd enjoy. I thought about it a long time. I kept telling myself: Do it! Go to London! And then I'd think: No. I'd be happy in London for six weeks, maybe less, and then I'd get restless and bored. I need my work. I can't cut myself off from that— it's most of what I have.

So, in my mind, I've been writing him a letter. A proposition is how I think of it. Come home, Jack. I love you. You can live with me and write your novel. I'll marry you, I'll support you (and Nancy and Tim and Laura and their goldfish and cats and dog and hamsters). But you'll have to live here, in New Jersey. New Jersey is perfect for me, the most crowded, neurotic, rootless state in the Union. My work is here and my roots are in my work.

Glancing at Mina's book just now, I come across a poem I hadn't remembered. It's called *Ancestors and Poetry*. In it she wanders through an old Dutch cemetery in Veddersburg. She says, walking there as a child, it seemed odd to her that the dust lying under the ground were her ancestors, had surely once been flesh and that they had lived, breathed, bled, begat. She was, she says, moved by them, indifferent to them, felt as unconnected to dead Van Duynes as if she were just passing through:

> *I'm a random speck*
>   *In a space and time*
>   *So fluid and combustible*
>   *I might as well never have been.*

The poem ends on a question. Was it to prove her own existence that she wrote poetry?

You're right, Mina, of course. Maybe we're all wanderers. Nothing lasts, we're all random specks, but while we're alive we ought to make the most of it.

Come home, Jack!

I love you.

I have a proposition for you.

If I write the letter, this is what I'll say.

T